Yurope: Hi]
By: Mich;
Copyright Michael Saint Wood 2012

Copyright: Michael Saint Wood
Published: Dec 23rd 2012
The right of Michael Saint Wood to be identified as author of this Work has been asserted by him in accordance with sections 77 and 78 of the Copyright, Designs and Patents Act of 1988.
All rights reserved. No part of this publication may be reproduced, stored in retrieval system, copied in any form or by any means, electronic, mechanical, photocopying, recording or otherwise transmitted without written permission from the author. You must not circulate this book in any format.

TRIGGER WARNING!
This novel contains strong language, violence, fat shaming, ableism, and cisgendered, heterosexual white men. Reading this novel may trigger painful recollections, imagined or otherwise, in the sensitive, socially aware, pseudo-intellectual, goo gobbling reader. In case this trigger warning has already triggered you, proceed to the nearest mirror, take a good hard look at yourself, then break the mirror and consume the broken glass. Hopefully, you'll get raped before bleeding out.
TRIGGER WARNING!

1.

Wicked winds tore at Thomas's naked body as he plummeted taint-first towards the sea. His dangling penis rotated counter-clockwise, like a veiny helicopter blade, but failed to propel him upwards. Thomas's testicles and anus billowed as he reached terminal velocity, but served him poorly as parachutes. Only a floating mound of hamburger wrappers preserved Thomas's life as he struck the undulating water. Bloody bubbles slipped between Thomas's fingers like red-hot rings as he sank. He awoke hours later, strapped to a metallic bed. Eighteen crusty, brown hamburger wrappers and a bloodied pair of tongs lay atop a blue trash bin near Thomas's head. The bin was otherwise filled to the brim with aborted fetuses. Brown fluid dripped across the white logo printed on the side of the bin, which depicted a rainbow colored fetus lying between two hamburger buns. A morbidly obese doctor leaned over Thomas, forcing rendered animal fat into Thomas's stomach via a feeding tube and syringe. A name-tag between the doctor's sweaty breasts displayed the first name Schlo, but the last name was obscured by a congealed chicken skin. As the doctor pressed his left hand against Thomas's right wrist, his doughy fingers produced a pleasant cushion sound. His crooked nose dug into Thomas's left shoulder and caked it with dried phlegm as he took Thomas's pulse. Wrinkles creased his forehead as he shoved a fistful of loose mayonnaise from his coat pocket into his own mouth. Then the doctor's pupils widened, like a cat peering into a darkened room.

"Damn it! He's starving. I need more cholesterol! Where the hell is that goy bastard Petit!" the doctor screamed while showering Thomas with rancid spittle.

A morbidly obese African American woman in a ranch dressing colored muumuu rolled into the room. Both of her shriveled, diabetes stricken feet hung from her backside like plump eggplants. The scent of fermenting coco butter filled the air as a fetus fell from a mottled slit between her festering feet and writhed on the urine stained tile floor.

"Sorry Doctor Mo, Doctor Petit's out getting a mandatory sex change," she said while tossing the doctor a tube of lard.

"Again? I thought we just hired a whole department of strong, independent, women that don't need no man," the doctor asked while shaking his head and snapping his free hand three times in a zigzag pattern.

"Yeah, but we didn't have enough dickless transsexuals," the nurse replied while biting through her umbilical chord, sucking out its contents, and tossing the deflated baby atop the bin filled with hamburger wrappers.

"Just like his forty seven brothers and sisters," she whispered as the brown infant wriggled in vain.

The infant clenched its delicate, wrinkled little hands and farted, filling the room with the acrid stench of secondhand soul food. The nurse retracted her head partially into her main bulk and began to laugh, causing her disgusting, rancid-milk scented breasts, backside, stomach, and colostomy bag to pulsate like a racing heart. As she laughed, the sinews that held her decaying feet in place snapped. As she rolled away, she grasped one of the feet and began to eat it. A toenail broke off between her teeth and she spat it down the hallway. The other foot stuck between two layers of her neck fat as she rolled over it and melded directly into her skin.

"That's too bad," the doctor whispered as the nurse rolled away, leaving a trail of bubbling backdoor booty butter in her wake. The doctor jammed the tube of lard into Thomas's mouth and continued, "She shouldn't have used the term 'dickless transsexual'. The phrase 'confused young lad interested in taking a load of piping hot prostate polliwogs in a hypothetical, festering, centipede infested axe wound where his inadequate penis currently resides' is much more socially acceptable. Besides, it's no fun when they snip off the dick. The smegma inside the fake snatch hole just doesn't taste the same. Sure, it is easier to spread on a bagel, but I find that it conflicts with the texture of the lox.

Thomas meant to vomit. He clawed his iron bed and passed out instead. Hundreds of needles pierced Thomas's flesh as he slept. He felt his limbs grow heavy and his pulse slow to a crawl. When he awoke seven days later, he took great labors just to breathe. Stretch marks covered his corpulent arms. His round, bulging stomach lay beneath a blanket emblazoned with the image of Jesus Christ in a red dress, drinking from a jar labeled "Lard Cola".

"You aren't reading that label I hope," a masculine voice called from across the room.

Thomas tried to sit up, but his body proved too heavy to lift. Little light penetrated the rusted grate ceiling of the cramped room Thomas inhabited. Uncountable barbecue sauce stains covered the floor.

"Literacy is against the law after all. You want to obey the law, don't you? Criminals have a nasty habit of disappearing in the lard mines these days," the voice continued.

"Where am I?" Thomas asked.

"You have immigrated to America. Welcome home," the voice replied.

"This is my home?"

"No, this is a holding cell. We can't just turn you loose

among red-blooded American citizens. While you pass the skin tone test, you arrived without identification and eighty pounds below the government-mandated minimum weight. We have taken measures to correct your health, but hot lard injections can only do so much. Don't you know how oppressive your former figure was? Just to look at you filled me with feelings of shame and regret. Now that you're of appropriate weight, neither of us has to face reality. Isn't that wonderful? Why, you're lucky you were taken to the hospital at the Israeli embassy. If you were taken to an American clinic, the automatic processing units would have denied you entry. That is, after the mandatory four month wait and after finding less than the minimum percentage of fluoride and pork fat in your blood. That being said, those Israelis have left you with a hefty bill. A lean against your future welfare credits is already in effect."

"What do you want from me?"

"That is a simple manner. All we require is evidence of your patriotism and ignorance. Educated men are often dangerous to society. They bring original ideas into the ghettos. Some of them even speak of rebellion against the state!"

The masculine voice chuckled as fluorescent light illuminated the room. Three long troughs filled with hamburgers lined the floor at Thomas's feet and sides. Beyond the trays, decaying corpses littered the floor. One corpse clutched a pistol and a moldy head of lettuce. Another clutched a paperback book and a blood spattered teddy bear.

"What is this?" Thomas asked in a raised, quavering voice.

"That is a very dangerous question," the voice replied. "A patriot knows better than to ask what or why. A patriot knows only how to consume and obey."

The clank of a cocking pistol sounded from the grated ceiling. Thomas nodded and grasped a hamburger with his trembling left hand. Three days passed before he finished the contents of all three troughs. Each time he began to retch, he turned his head towards a grating in the floor. By the time he finished his meal, the basin below his chambers stunk of vomit and liquid feces.

"I'm finished," Thomas whispered as the final bite disappeared into his stomach.

"Not quite yet," the masculine voice replied.

Two years passed in a tortured blur. Each morning, hooded figures filled Thomas's cell with junk food, healthy food, picture books, televisions, novels, and writing materials. Any time Thomas utilized the writing materials, consumed the healthy food, or even glanced at the novels, the hooded men would beat him within an inch of his life. Thomas expected that simply eating the junk food, feigning ignorance, and temporarily abandoning expressing his thoughts would be enough to end his confinement. Only absolute surrender could save him. As those two years passed, Thomas began to crave the junk food. In fact, when a vegetable was secretly sneaked into his macaroni and cheese milkshake, he covered the floor with syrupy orange vomit. The idea of reading became repugnant to him. If a single letter was to flash across the screen of his television, he would scream and look away. Thoughts fell behind a veil of hunger, hatred, and thirst. Near the end of that second year, Thomas fell into a fever. At first, he imagined that the world was spinning, then he realized he was being rolled out of the cell and across cracking pavement. Salt air felt cool against his bulging stomach. Each time Thomas rotated, he risked suffocating on his own tremendous bulk. Each time his head reached the twelve o'clock position, he gasped for that salted air, not because he wanted to breathe, but because his body craved the salt. As Thomas rolled to the edge of a precipice, clattering footfalls sounded in the distance.

"Is he ready?" a female asked.

"Let's find out," the masculine voice from before replied.

An overstuffed boot struck Thomas's rounded backside. Sand stuck between his fat folds as he rolled downhill. White flashes seared the sky as Thomas rolled to a stop. Something irresistible radiated aroma inches from his face.

"He is ready," the male voice rasped as Thomas began to consume the tray of cheeseburgers laid before him.

That male voice cackled, then began to cough. The sound of a plump hand striking against a male breast sounded. The whirring of strained electric wheelchair motors followed. As Thomas consumed the mound of burgers, seven other persons consumed the man that spoke to Thomas in his cell. Thomas passed out in a fit of diabetic shock, then awoke three hours later in a dimly lit room. His first thought was a craving for baby back ribs. His second was an urge to scream.

"What have they done to me?" he whispered.

Something cold and rigid pressed against Thomas's crown. Condensation dripped across his aching forehead. Thomas turned towards that object and lapped up the fluid. Try as he might, Thomas could neither stand, nor turn over. As he struggled, muffled whistling sounded from the space he assumed his feet would be. He lay in, what he later discovered to be a bed, for the next several weeks. He wiggled his fingers and toes, consuming only condensation from the basin at the head of his bed. As his body burned fat for fuel, Thomas began to flail his wrists and ankles, then his entire arms and legs. At the end of his third month of fasting, Thomas stood from his bed, sickly, but only twenty pounds overweight. He leaned forward and washed his face in the sink at the head of his bed. The water tasted greasy, like bacon fat, and left his fingers shimmering like perfectly cooked hotdogs. Thomas spat, then looked towards the foot of his bed. There, hundreds of aluminum cans littered the floor. A muffled whistle blew between the cans. Pressing the cans aside, Thomas watched another can float up through the basin of a toilet. He reached down and grasped that can. As he had yet to move his bowels since arriving in his new apartment, Thomas found the water palatable and free of rendered fat. As he held the can to his face to study the label, he noticed light reflecting across its surface. Peering across the room, Thomas noticed an illuminated screen built into an adjacent wall. The screen depicted an elderly Caucasian man in a three-piece suit eating a bowl full of mixed animal penises. Preteen Chinese girls threw beanbags at him while he ate, attempting to knock him off his yoga ball and into a pit of lava below. Thomas's pupils dilated. He then began to giggle and lightly clap his hands. Peering down at his hands, he shook his head violently and clenched his fingers into plump, bacon-scented fists. Wondering how he had gone so long without noticing the screen or at least hearing it, he reached up either hand and felt his ears. Moldy particles of hamburger buns crumbled at the touch of Thomas's fingers. He heard clearly, though not without slight discomfort.

"I was a prisoner of war in Korea you heartless bitches!" the man on the screen barked before biting into a boiled elephant labia. "They used to dress me up like the Skipper from Gilligan's Island. Each day, a little Korean man dressed like Gilligan followed me in order to sabotage any attempt I made to escape. I had to stay in character and call him little buddy or I would have been executed on the spot! At the end of every week, that Korean man would dress up as either Mary Anne or Ginger. I then had to make sweet, passionate love to him while staying in character. If I failed to please the little Korean man or fell out of my hammock, I would have to start all over, with him dressed like Mrs. Howell! Do you have any idea how painful it is to titty fuck two coconut halves? My dick looks like burnt gum!"

As Thomas considered replacing the hamburger buns in his ears, he spotted a door beyond the screen and decided to step outside. Standing for the first time in three months proved laborious enough, walking sent Thomas's senses spiraling. He pressed through his doorway and down a long hallway that seemed to tremble beneath his feet. Cold air struck Thomas from a staircase that he could not see. Leaning forward, he plummeted down sturdy stairs. Someone helped him to his feet. Another person pressed him against a wall.

"The new tenant, huh?" a gruff voice asked.

"Looks like his blood sugar's low," a belching female voice replied.

Fat, greasy fingers pressed against Thomas's lower mandible. An entire five-liter bottle of Doritos flavored Mountain Dew poured down his throat and all over his red, white, and blue muumuu.

"You can thank me later handsome," the female voice continued while giving Thomas a playful slap on the penis.

He recoiled in fear and struck something solid. That object rotated counterclockwise and flung Thomas onto cracked pavement. He peered up, feeling soda sugar surging through his veins. His eyes focused. Flickering neon lights came into view. Advertisements covered not only the exterior of the building Thomas exited, but also the entire sky. A neon baby ate a neon burger. Two buns appeared around the baby and a larger neon baby consumed the first. Thomas turned to his left and hurried down the path. Despite the lights overhead, the road seemed dreadfully dim. Amber lights flickered from thin windows as American citizens pressed their foreheads against illuminated screens. One such person turned towards Thomas as Thomas stumbled past the window and screamed for him to "get out of shape weirdo!" Thomas peered down at his bulging stomach and decided to try sprinting. Two morbidly obese men in semen stained, floral print dresses lay on the side of the road, some two hundred paces away at the peak of a hill, punching each other in the testicles and weeping. As Thomas sprinted uphill, their conversation echoed towards him.

"As an enlightened, liberated, failure-as-a-man-sexual, I believe deep down, in the heart of my bottom, that I am the same as any woman, man, child, lizard, or black person. But I also realize that, through my trials and tribulations of life that I have never once queefed."

The person speaking paused as though overcome with emotion. He embraced the other cross-dressing man, causing their neck stubble to intertwine.

"I feel your pain bro-sister," the other man replied. "How can we be equal if we've never queefed? Women can climb mountains. They can play football, and have abortions. Now I've never had an abortion but I'd like to think I do my part when I dump my used syringes at the playground. But I have never released the gaseous form of my inner feminist while reciting non-rhyming poetry and storing the fallout in a mason jar to smell later while thinking about my father, whom I resent. It just makes me feel so empty inside, like there's a place within me reserved for a queef, but wasted on a prostate and my massive smelly testicles!"

Thomas's footfalls drowned out the chatter of cross-dressing men. They both frowned as he sprinted past.

"Look at that ablest pig!" one of them screamed.

"I'd call the Hurt Feelings Police if I wasn't so busy hating men!" the other replied.

"Yeah, I hate men so much, especially my father, whom I resent, that I want to dress like a woman and have loving, nurturing, balls-deep sex in the shitter with him, I mean them!"

Thomas peered back, towards the raised voices, and tripped. Flecks of dried butter collected on his muumuu as he rolled down a hill. When he came to a stop, he stood and vomited soda and stomach acid into a storm drain. Three children, each of which clutched a fetus, rushed to drink Thomas's vomit, and to feed the fetuses they carried.

"Thank you sir," one of them whispered, before retreating into a dark corner of the sewer.

Thomas shook his head and looked away. Burger shops and coffee lounges lined either side of the road. At the far end however, a row of sandbags blocked the entrance to a decrepit building composed near entirely of glass. Bright yellow badges pinned to each sandbag depicted an open novel overlaid atop the standard radioactivity warning sign. Thomas lumbered forward and rolled over the barrier. As he entered the building, a smile spread across his face. Hundreds of worm eaten books lay across the floor of the abandoned library. Thomas remembered what he had heard of the illegality of literacy and proceeded forward with the utmost caution. He sprinted into a shadow and looked in every direction while catching his breath. Thomas thought of what he meant to read and what would be most beneficial for him to study.

"What is this place called America?" he thought first. Then, "Why am I here, or rather, how did I get here? And now that I think about it, where the hell did I come here from?"

Thomas remembered that his name was Thomas. He remembered falling to a floor, waking among the clouds, yelling angrily at someone, shoving them, and falling from a great height.

"Everything before that is a blur," he said aloud.

Dozens of windows flickered with the reflections of neon light. Thomas turned back to address the contents of the shelf he leaned against. He saw first a row of classics. Though he recalled little about his circumstances, the works of Homer and Dumas inspired vivid recollections of their contents. Thomas read the spine of every novel on the shelf, all of which were paperbacks, save for one. A coffee table type book jutted horizontally from the bookcase, as though hastily wedged in by some thoughtless patron. Thomas retrieved the hardback book and smiled upon perceiving the title. He meant to sit down and read immediately; however, breaking glass disturbed his thoughts.

"Who is that?" Thomas asked while looking all around.

Amber light flared by the entrance and flickered across dozens of broken windows.

"Take that, you CIS-gendered, oppressive, seductive pig!" a gruff voice called out.

Thomas ran towards the front doors, but two lit Molotov cocktails crashed through the glass and filled the atrium with flames. Black, writhing smoke permeated the library. Thomas sprinted towards an exit, but became dizzy and unable to see the way. He wandered burning hallways lined with books and struggled to breathe. Panting, trembling, he fell to the floor. Thomas awoke later the following morning. The neon lights overhead had switched from projecting a pale, moonlight color, to an amber hue, like that of a rising sun. Directly above Thomas, the neon image of the American flag flickered on and off in a poor imitation of a waving cloth. The stars and stripes our readers may be familiar with were absent. In their place, fifty-four hamburgers and thirteen horizontal crucifixes shimmered as though on fire. Thomas peered first left, then right. The library lay in ruins. Only Thomas's flame retardant muumuu had preserved his life. Shattered glass sparkled in every direction like uncountable stars. Thomas sat up and smirked, every book, save for the one he held had been destroyed in the fire.

"The American Architectural De-Revolution," Thomas read aloud from the cover.

Though he could not remember why, the thought of architecture lit a flame in his soul. The first several pages depicted beautiful buildings that dated back to the Victorian era. Beyond those pages, only drab gray cubes appeared. Thomas frowned and turned back towards the beginning. According to the captions he read, all American buildings had been forcibly converted into plain square cubes two years earlier so no one would have to feel jealous of another person's circumstances. Even the Grey Cube House, formerly known as the Whitehouse, was converted. Castles, towers, and beautiful statues flashed before Thomas's eyes as though for the first time. Each time he turned the page, the novel deteriorated slightly. By the time he reached the final page, the spine snapped and the pages fell like confetti. Particles of the old world slipped between Thomas's trembling fingers. He then peered down at his stomach and frowned.

"I have to make this right," he decided aloud.

2.

Sirens echoed. The amber lights overhead flickered brilliantly before fading. Burnt ozone left Thomas light headed. Peering across the sea of shattered glass where the library once stood, Thomas noticed four morbidly obese children watching him from the semen stained windows of a grey cube building. A splintered crucifix covered in advertisements for Mo-Luster brand pole wax flickered in candlelight behind them. Fog poured from their snout-like noses, obscuring their rounded features and recently tussled hair. As Thomas waved at the children, brilliant light illuminated his fingers.

"Literacy alert, literacy alert, all citizens must report to their entertainment squares for roll call!" a strained voice blared from unseen loudspeakers.

The light on Thomas's hand focused until it formed a powerful cone as a tremendous motor sounded in the distance. As Thomas peered over the grey roof of the church, three helicopters came into view. As they sped towards Thomas, they seemed to flicker red, white, and blue. Thomas sprinted forward several steps, lost his footing, and rolled into an alley. Half-asleep and drunken citizens lined the alley like cholesterol in a sluggish artery. Sausagey fingers, pneumatic grabber claws, and semi-sentient colostomy bags reached towards him, but Thomas proved too slippery with sweat to grasp. A mass of bodies stood across from the alley, near the entrance of a tremendous grey building. Thomas rolled into that crowd just as the tremendous gray doors slid open.

"Are you here for the monthly 'Approved Speech Hour' or the circle jerk in the alley out back?" a shrill voice inquired as Thomas rolled to a stop.

Thomas peered up with rotating eyes. Masses of undulating flesh poured into the dreary cubed building. To the right of the entrance, red-faced men in motorized wheelchairs rolled into an alley. One poor soul with a burned out engine struggled to manually spin his wheels. Due to the lubrication dripping from his fingers, his chair merely wobbled in place. This man peered back at Thomas and smiled.

"Lend me a hand?" he asked with a wink.

Thomas cringed and looked away.

"Good, I didn't want to walk in alone," the shrill voice continued. "And the other guys at the circle jerks always want to spoon afterwards. It's like a dog licking it's own balls, not because it feels good; trust me, I know from experience exactly how good it feels to lick a dogs balls; but because they like the taste!"

Two meaty hands clasped Thomas by his flabby breasts and helped him to his feet. Acrid breath permeated Thomas's nostrils as he peered into a pair of beady, seemingly lifeless eyes. The man before him stood without a walker or a cane, but his barrel shaped stomach dwarfed Thomas's by a factor of three. Matted brown hair hung in loose curls around his leathery neck, ears, and butt-cheeks. Rancid sweat poured between his prematurely graying eyebrows, down a nose that resembled an overripe tomato, and onto a magnificently thick mustache that twitched as he spoke. A viscous white substance dripped from the hem of his purple tube-top, mixing with the puss oozing from the numerous sores on his exposed stomach. His left hand remained on Thomas's breast. His right reached out to clasp Thomas's left hand.

"My name is Joe. Pleased to meet you. I'd tell you more about me, but the guys at the Reprogramming Camp wiped out most of my memory to make room for tolerance, acceptance, and subliminal commercials for lard infused soda that appear every time I blink."

"I'm pretty sure my name is Thomas. Nice to meet you Joe," Thomas replied.

Something about this stranger left Thomas ill at ease. Perhaps it was the way Joe's eyes darted from left to right. Perhaps it was the steam emitting from the massive bulge in the front of his lime green thong. For a moment, Thomas considered turning away. Helicopter blades whirred overhead, causing the gummy tissues that lined the pavement to stir. Thomas nodded and entered the building instead. Dead ahead, hundreds of Americans rolled into hydraulically reinforced beanbag chairs opposite of a plain grey stage obscured by plain grey curtains. A smell like boiling urine struck Thomas suddenly. As he wretched and leaned against a plain gray wall, his right elbow pressed against the back a grunting woman. Looking over, Thomas saw that she sat precariously atop a semi-transparent container bolted the wall.

"Lend a hand?" she asked.

"How?" Thomas replied.

"Just turn the crank on the side of the box," she replied between gasping breaths.

Something cried within the box as Thomas turned the crank. Then a sound like macerating meat, a sizzle, and a whistle similar to the one built into Thomas's toilet followed. The woman sighed and leaned forward, catching herself against Joe's right bosom.

"Are you going to eat that?" he asked.

"Help yourself," she replied while lighting a match and waving it in the air.

"What the heck was that all about?" Thomas asked as the woman walked away.

As Joe kneeled before the container, Thomas finally noticed the silhouette of an infant resting between two hamburger buns painted just above the crank. Joe reached into a compartment in the container and retrieved two hamburgers wrapped in blue paper.

"What are the odds, twin boys!" he exclaimed while handing a burger to Thomas.

Putrid heat seeped through the wrapper. As Joe led Thomas towards two vacant chairs, the burger fell from his hand. Glittering stage lights stunned all onlookers. As Joe tore into his free meal, a megaphone descended towards the stage via a metallic cord and pulley.

"Ladies and gentlemen," a commanding female voice began.

"Excuse me, but I am neither a lady nor a gentleman!" a minuscule Asian man in the front row interrupted while standing.

Spotlights illuminated the ruffled shoulders of his orange Sunday-dress. His curly afro wig slid to the side as he continued.

"My name is Ngo Dong and your blatant misuse of pronouns both offends me and grants me this opportunity to garner attention for myself!"

"Pardon me Ngo, what pronouns would you prefer?" the disembodied voice replied as the megaphone twirled from left to right, as though shaking its head disgustedly.

"Though I prefer the term 'strong independent black

woman that don't need no man', the term 'special snowflake' will suffice."

"Hello ladies, gentlemen, and mentally ill products of repeated child molestation. Welcome to this month's 'Approved Speech Hour' brought to you by DiaBread-ic, the bread based prosthetic foot that you can eat! Before we begin, I would like to bring out the least privileged person in all America to say a few words about privilege."

Retracting gray curtains revealed a cock-eyed abomination. A smegma-encrusted yarmulke hung from a football-sized tumor protruding from the back of its bowling pin shaped head. Its distended stomach peeked through layers of a yellowed wedding dress, revealing a mottled, seventeen-inch long outie belly button. Puffy, cupcake-like nipples dribbled grey liquid that mixed with the steaming sweat of its armpits and neck folds. The creature appeared to walk from left to right across a stage. Upon closer inspection, Thomas noticed the airplane landing gear bolted to each of its undulating butt-cheeks. Liquid feces dripped from its pitch-black fingers as it grasped the megaphone. Its shadow cast a pall across the stage.

"Before my stint at the reprogramming camp," the creature began in a pained, dying-whale-like voice, "I was a privileged white mother of two who dared to question the government's authority to grind my daughters into hamburger patties and reprogram my husband into becoming a full-on butt-loving spooch-mooching homosexual. Now that I'm a proud, morbidly obese, trans-religious, chromosomally enhanced, black man with a soul full of jazz music and three smelly testicles full of all known strains of hepatitis, I understand the need for political correctness and the political correcting provided here at the monthly Approved Speech Hour."

An applause sign lit above the orator. Thomas meant to clap half heartedly, but Joe stayed his hands. Clattering noises sounded near that sign as a single woman in the back of the theater clapped, then cursed after realizing her mistake. A muffled burst sent the stage curtains on end. The woman recoiled then fell to the floor dead.

"Applause!" a booming female voice demanded from the megaphone.

The audience obeyed, clapping hands like clackers composed of rotting plums. The thing bent at the middle, causing a solid wave of grease to fall from its forehead, then rolled backwards with trembling hands obscuring its bulging eyes. The megaphone dangled momentarily, then twisted to point towards the audience.

"I would like to begin my lecture with a list of things you must never say," its booming, feminine voice began. "The first thing you must never say is, well, I don't know exactly how to tell you not to say it, as it's something that I'm not even allowed to say myself."

"Oh I know what to do!" special snowflake Ngo interrupted.

He bounded onto the stage and grasped the microphone with both hands.

"Just say it in a hypothetical sense. For instance, the first thing you must never say is," Ngo began.

Clattering noises followed by a second muffled burst interrupted the speech. Pink mist hung in the air as Ngo crumpled to the floor. Thomas meant to stand from his beanbag chair, but Joe held him fast in place with a hand as firm as his erection.

"Why did you shoot him?" a man demanded while

bounding towards the stage.

"He was about to say something politically incorrect," the female voice of the megaphone replied.

The interloper brushed past Thomas and clambered onto the stage. Improper lighting obscured his torso. The slow falling mist of blood settled on the wide brimmed hat that obscured his face. Angry voices began to clatter, but all in attendance fell silent as the interloper began to speak.

"How are Americans supposed to know what not to say if they can not even discuss it hypothetically? Are they to live in fear, apathetic to the world they inhabit?"

"Works for me," the booming voice replied

Clattering sounded again from the catwalk, but the voice continued.

"No, let this fool speak. Let him see how American's respond when confronted with unapproved speech."

Ngo groaned while writhing on the floor. Blood poured from the bullet hole above his heart, mixing with tufts of his wiry chest hair.

"Yeah, don't man-splain to me you privileged white freak," he whispered.

The megaphone lowered towards his lips as he continued.

"What do you know about the American struggle? Living life as a straight white male is like playing a video game on easy mode."

"Who told you what it's like to be straight, one of your

dads?" the interloper interrupted with an air of disgust.

"Yes!" Ngo replied. "I've lived my entire life on a razor's edge. If I live like a traditional Asian, I'm told that I'm a stereotype. If I act like everyone else, they call me a banana. You know, yellow on the outside and white on the inside? What choice did I have but to become a proud, independent black woman that don't need no man?"

"Don't be silly Ngo. You're not an Asian stereotype. And you're nothing like a banana."

"I'm not?"

"No, you're more like a public toilet, yellow on the outside and full of shit."

Members of the audience began to interject, but the interloper continued unabated.

"Don't you think, after all that, it's wrong of you to judge me based on the color of my skin? It's not like I'm even white. I just have a skin condition that makes my skin this color. I inherited it from my parents who both inherited it from their parents and so on. How dare you discriminate against me due to my affliction? I don't even know how you can sleep at night."

"On a pillow covered in bite marks!" Ngo rasped.

Seven members of the audience chuckled and were promptly shot. The interloper grasped the brim of his hat, then continued.

"Listen Ngo, I get that you want to be a brown person, but being full of shit is not the way to go about it. You have confused having a cunt with being one, and I don't use that word lightly, as cunts tend to find it offensive."

"I bet you think you're so clever with your micro-aggressions."

"Maybe you would prefer some macro aggression!" the interloper cried while cocking back his right leg at an odd angle.

Something about the voice struck Thomas as familiar. As the interloper's boot collided with Ngo's backside, the brim of his hat lifted. In that brief moment of anger and fear, Thomas and the interloper met eyes.

"That's enough of your nonsense Kuzen. Bring him in!" the feminine voice of the megaphone announced.

Eight security guards in extra large bulletproof vests descended towards the interloper on steel cables. Half of the cables snapped, causing four of those men to plummet through the stage. The remaining four struck the stage with a thud as an intricate catwalk collapsed upon them. The interloper recoiled, heading for the back of the stage. As screams filled the theater, Thomas stood reflexively. Though he had not thought to do so, his body intended to follow that man. Joe grabbed for him and missed. As Thomas reached towards the stage, the butt of a rifle sailed over his head.

"No one told you homos to leave," a guard rasped while struggling to keep from falling off the stage.

"He isn't gay!" Joe replied as the guard fell on top of Thomas.

The guard grasped Thomas by the back of the neck and pressed Thomas's face against the sticky linoleum floor.

"I don't see a waiver tattoo behind your left ear faggo. It's the Ministry of Buggery for the both of you!" the guard cried.

Thomas meant to interject, but a second guard fell on top of the first, sending Thomas into feverish dreams. When Thomas awoke hours later, he found himself sitting opposite a frowning man.

"I am sorry sir, but I must insist that you become a homosexual. It's no big deal really, just a bit of balls deep spooning twice a week. Oh, and you'll have to grow a mustache," the man sitting opposite of Thomas began.

He wore a tight black bow-tie that seemed to be painted onto his massive, pack-of-hot-dogs-like neck. Grease dripped from his slicked back hair onto the supple leather of his gargantuan office chair, which Thomas struggled to distinguish from his well tanned, yet crusty and completely naked body.

"But I like girls," Thomas replied while rubbing his temples.

"Nonsense boy, that is just your selfish white nature speaking. You see, mandatory homosexuality not only benefits society by deflating that pesky white population, what with their inadequate butt-cheeks, straight hair, and insistence on being able to read, but it also frees up more young gash for the rest of us. And do forgive me for being blunt, but at your current sub standard levels of corpulence, you could have any cross eyed woman you desired."

"Why cross eyed?"

"Because she'd be seeing me on the side you silly goose. That's a little joke. We like to keep things loose around here. Speaking of which, please turn around and bend over. I am required to calibrate your circumference."

As the interviewer spoke, he stood, retrieved a jar of grape jelly from his desk and began to rub the contents all over his chest and testicles. Thomas stood and meant to run towards the door located directly behind his chair. As he turned back however, the door flew open, sending shards of dried grape jelly across Thomas's chest.

"I am sorry Thomas, but I cannot wait in line another second," Joe said between gasps of breath.

"What is the meaning of this sir? I have extremely urgent matters to attend!" the naked man replied while placing the empty jelly jar atop his erect penis.

"I demand that you register me as a reverse lesbian this instant!" Joe replied. "It will help me meet girls with low standards and look, I already have breasts!"

"Yes but your breasts are hairy and lumpy and gross and smell like a wet dog anus."

"I will remind you that I'm applying to become a lesbian."

"Fair enough. To be perfectly honest, I'm a little intrigued by your proposal. Thomas, would you be so kind as to wait in the lobby? I'll get back to you later."

As Thomas brushed past Joe, he mouthed "Thank you", and Joe replied with a nod, a knowing wink, and a fart that smelled exactly like strawberries. Thomas peered across the lobby at four men reclining on overstuffed sofas. An entertainment square on the opposite wall displayed live coverage of a school shooting. A reporter from Rolling Stone followed the young shooter, asking him about his favorite bands and whether or not he was single. A young girl appeared in frame and was promptly blown to pieces. The interviewer smiled and quipped that she found a completely new way to give explosive head. Thomas stumbled forward, his head spinning and his stomach ready to empty in reverse. An immense, stick bug resembling transsexual in a lime green bikini stood up from his desk. Dim light glimmered atop the shemale pattern baldness induced bare spot on the top of his head. Three jheri-curled hairs dangled from his madams apple as he turned to face Thomas. From the smell of this person, Thomas couldn't tell whether they were african-american or if every inch of their body was covered in feces

"I think I need to use the bathroom," Thomas muttered.

The pungent man led Thomas down a narrow hall, towards a series of doors marked with odd paintings. The first door was marked with a turtle wearing a wedding dress, the second, a potted plant in a wheel chair, the third, a cartoon ghost, and the fourth, the baby burger logo.

"Do you have to pump a dump out of your plump little rump, rebuke the spook with your penis puke, or coat hanger a baby?" the receptionist asked. "I mean, abortions are normally just for the girls, but we don't discriminate here. You know, except against straight white men. If you feel entitled to an abortion, just head behind the door with the baby burger logo and a privileged white infant will be provided for you. Now of course, if you're looking to alleviate and deviate that prostate post haste, head through the door with the sexy turtle logo. There you'll find a sophisticated virtual reality headset and a lukewarm holiday ham with the bone pulled out.

"Just leave me alone," Thomas replied.

He meant to say more but felt his stomach turn. His hands felt incredibly hot as he reached forward and grabbed the handle of the nearest door. The receptionist sighed and peered back his desk. There, a pair of bloated testicles lay at the bottom of a fish tank otherwise occupied by suckerfish with cold-sores on their lips. As his footfalls echoed down the hallway, Thomas felt each step reverberate off the tiled bathroom wall. A crusty brown sink stood three paces ahead. Turning to his right, Thomas found the light switch inoperable. Two filthy bathroom stalls occupied the corner opposite of the sink. Thomas approached the nearest stall and slipped inside. His forehead felt grotesquely damp with sweat. He reached down for some toilet paper to dab it with, but grabbed something rigid and pulsating instead. Melting plastic bubbled against the outer edge of the thing. Red-hot light poured between Thomas's fingers like luminous rings.

As he peered down at the glowing tube clutched in his trembling hand, a voice on the wind rasped, "Oooh, I'm the glory hole ghost. Now let me plop a drop in that dank booty stank before I haunt you!"

"Wait a second," Thomas replied "A real ghost penis would be non corporeal and would just slip right into my body!"

The voice instantly replied, "That's kind of the idea, oooooh!"

Thomas furrowed his brow and pressed an ear against the inner partition wall.

"Is that you Joe?" he asked in a voice both inquisitive and furious.

The voice replied, "What, no! I'm not the handsome stranger Joe you just met and owe a favor to. Not that there's anything wrong with Joe hypothetically finding you attractive. Who are you to judge Joe you stupid homophobic asshole, which by the way is the only variety of asshole I dislike!"

"God damn it Joe, get out of that stall and put away your

weird, glowing dick!"

　　Before the voice in the other stall could reply, Thomas grimaced and snapped the glowing member in a ninety-degree angle to ensure that the supposed ghost could not escape. Lights flickered on and off again in as Thomas pressed open his own stall door with the back of his right shoulder. Fluorescent light glittered across uncountable, piss yellow tiles as Thomas kicked down the bathroom door. He sprinted through numerous identical hallways until he found an exit, then sprinted down numerous identical streets until he reached his apartment. Two months passed in relative peace, during which Thomas became better acclimated to his new life in America.

3.

Thomas slumbered silently in his luxurious twin sized bed. It was the second best bed allowance credits could buy and built by only the finest quality Chinese children. Thomas's feet hung in the air above the government appointed toilet at the foot of his bed. His forehead pressed against the cold, yellowed, porcelain basin of his government appointed kitchen sink. Thomas rolled over and kicked at his government appointed red white and blue blankets. He dreamed of running across a large stretch of silvery water. Amber light struck him from a golden spire in the distance. Thomas looked up and shielded the powerful light with his hand. Crimson embers crept between his pinky and middle fingers, then faded. Thomas lowered his hand and peered back at the tower. A shadowy figure stood atop the tower in a brown robe lined with yellow fur. A strange voice wafted up the cracked plastic siding of Thomas's apartment complex and tore him from his dream.

"I finally found you!" the shrill voice cried.

Thomas saw first the off-white ceiling of his bedroom. He perceived three water spots from the upstairs tenant's leaky toilet as well as one semen stain that he could not account for. He threw his red white and blue blankets aside and slipped on his government appointed fuzzy slippers. Static electricity built on Thomas as he shuffled across his faded shag carpet; causing his filthy ass hairs to stand on end like a colonic cowlick. Daylight struck Thomas's feet as he approached his window. A government mandated framed photograph of a cheeseburger fell over as he leaned outside.

"Was someone calling me?" Thomas asked.

"Yes you!" the shrill voice responded.

Thomas looked first to his left, where a morbidly obese

man slept atop the most finely crafted, luxurious dumpster in the area. Thomas then looked to his right where he saw Joe in a frilly pink dress.

"How dare you oppress me?" Joe said while shaking a purple rhinestone encrusted pixie wand in Thomas's direction.

"Me, oppress you? I'm hardly even know you," Thomas replied.

"Oh, yes you do Mister! You and everyone like you oppress me by denying me the right to marry another man!"

Joe held his forehead with his feces encrusted palm, attempting to hold back his tears. Purple sequins fell from his shoulders onto his purple high-heeled shoes where they stuck to a layer of caked on black tar and semen.

"No, really. I'm all for your kind of person marrying," Thomas replied.

Joe paused for a moment, as though calculating his maneuver.

"So you'll marry me then?" he asked.

Blush spread across his cheeks and also his face. Slobber dripped from the corners of his mustache and fell between his flabby breasts.

"Goodness no!" Thomas replied.

Joe snapped his pixie wand in half and stomped so hard he broke the heel of his left shoe.

"I should have known this would happen. Look everyone, this man is a racist, fascist, right wing, left handed, big nosed bigot!" he screamed.

"Don't you think you're over reacting?" Thomas asked while covering his nose with his left hand. "I mean, I hardly know you. It doesn't seem right to marry someone I just met."

"Oh!" Joe called sarcastically to the crowd of disheveled onlookers that gathered outside of Thomas's window. "Listen here everyone. This man thinks I'm not good enough for him. What kind of country are we living in where a man in a frilly dress can not force another man to marry him, support him, love him, shave him, peel the lesions off his back and eat them?"

"Hillary will fix him!" a woman dressed in a grey fur tube top called out.

"Yes, our champion Hillary levels all inequalities!" an elderly black man with his pants around his ankles replied.

Thomas intended to interject, but the crowd drowned out his rebuttal by chanting "Hillary, Hillary!" and Thomas retreated into his bedroom in great confusion. He sat down on the edge of his bed to gather his wits. A bead of sweat fell from Thomas's short brownish hair onto his soiled government issued underpants. Thomas hung back his head and breathed in deeply. His apartment stunk. No, it was the entire neighborhood the reeked of ignorance, injustice, debauchery, and also shit.

"I have to get out of this place." Thomas decided.

He made ready to stand. Before he was fully erect however, a knock sounded at his door. Thomas threw on his only clean clothing that fit; a faded brown suit with a threadbare black tie he found two weeks earlier in an abandoned laundromat.

"I'll be right there!" Thomas called out.

"Don't worry about it," a male voice replied.

Thomas heard rustling as he slipped on his scuffed brown boots. Looking forward, he saw a yellowed piece of paper slip beneath his door. Thomas stepped over his toilet and passed the entertainment area, which was composed of a twelve by twelve inch panel in the wall where government mandated entertainment played at all hours of the day. Thomas usually kept it obscured, but the cardboard cover he made out of his government mandated bible had fallen off during the night and he had no way to turn off the sound. As Thomas approached the front door, he looked to his left to see a morbidly obese woman clapping her ham shaped hands as a shirtless male athlete shoveled lard into her gaping maw.

"Same shit as yesterday," Thomas mumbled as he stuck the cardboard cover back in place.

"We try our best!" a nasally voice replied from the intercom integrated into the entertainment square.

Thomas squatted by the front door. Yellow light poured in through the void between the door bottom and the hallway floor. His hairy knuckles tore three chips of peeling white paint from the doorframe as he grasped the paper. He took three steps back and sat on his toilet. A small whistle sounded from the top of the toilet. Thomas spread his legs as a can of government approved breakfast foods floated up through the toilet basin. The can was about six inches in height and three inches diameter. The label depicted an obese, sassy black female Jesus lactating entire corncobs with one disgusting mottled breast and dark yellow butter with the other.

"Corn shell cakes again?" Thomas mumbled as he lifted the can from the stinking water.

Thomas sniffed his allotted rations and grimaced before tossing the can over his shoulder. It landed on a pile on the other side of his bed. The twice-folded piece of paper in Thomas's hand felt oddly heavy. Thomas wiped his left hand on his pants leg before unfolding the paper.

"Meet me at the Hillary Clinton rally today at noon. I have something very important to show you," Thomas read aloud. "Something important, what could that mean? How did they know I could read and why didn't they sign their name?" he wondered.

As if on cue, Hillary Clinton appeared on Thomas's entertainment square. She held a book in one hand and a lit match in the other. The title of the book read "Free thought". Cold orange light struck Thomas's cheek as he contemplated his decision. As the flames faded, images of obese women rolling naked in hamburgers covered the screen as a nasally voice detailed Hillary's rise to president elect. Thomas did his best to look away as the news story began to play.

"As we all know, following the disappearance of President Barack 'Hussein in the Membrane' Obama, a disgusting heterosexual white male colluded with Russians to replace him. Fortunately, after months of controversy, that privileged shitlord found it in his heart to commit suicide by shooting himself twice in the back of the head. Following this, former president Bill Clinton spent half of the last year of his life bribing, I mean, appealing to congress to grant him a third term as interim president. Shortly following his re-institution, Bill perished during a five-day long bubble bath. He entered the bath with two meatball hoagies, a bottle of wine, and a mixtape of his favorite saxophone solos. After consuming the first hoagie, he became far too full of freedom to exit the tub. His wife Hillary brought a proposal to congress and congress voted to create a panel to discuss whether or not pulling the president from the tub was fiscally responsible. His presence in the tub, some argued, raised the tub's water efficiency level and hundreds of Big Macs remained uneaten in his absence. That panel then went through several votes as how best to react to the president's plight, how funds should be raised to enact their plan, and whose turn it was to pay for lunch. Of course, it was the taxpayer's turn to pay every time. The president died of starvation on the fifth day of deliberations. He lost enough weight to leave the tub on the third day, but his fingers were pruny and he could not hold a grip on his porcelain casket. Other persons present could have helped him exit the tub, but most thought it would be gay to touch a naked man while a mixtape of jazz music played. Of course, as we all know, one out of every five white males are mandated to be gay, castrated, or fans of soft jazz music by law, but all present were either minorities or had previously attained waivers."

"Following the President's death, a panel of four persons, chosen via the top internet search engine queries shared the power of presidency in his place. After eliminating all porn stars, libertarians, and Dennis Kucinich, that panel included a white rapper, a young girl with a terminal illness, a very cute kitten, and the ghost of Ronald Reagan. The white rapper "Willy Welfare" proved the most influential of the group, immediately pushing forward legislation for free food delivered via the toilet. As he put it, 'All my homeys need is love, respect, free food, and a place to shit.' Terminally ill Rebecca, as she often called herself, was the second most influential of the group. She called for mandatory tea parties with the very cute kitten each day in the grey cubed building formerly known as the Whitehouse. Terminally Ill Rebecca passed no other legislation during her term in office. When questioned on her stances of social issues, she often remarked, 'I am dying. I am a precious little girl and I am going to die. Like me on face book, as doing so is equivalent to one prayer, then leave me alone you heartless cunt.' Ronald Reagan's ghost rarely appeared in public. Often, only the sound of trickling economics gave hint to his presence. Despite his constant absence, he somehow managed to raise taxes seven thousand percent on the middle class."

"Fortunately, at that point in American history, the middle class was comprised entirely of a balding Caucasian man named Henry Shackleford. The remaining portion of the population was either part on the multi trillionaire one percent, a member of the non working class, sold to China as cheap cat food filler, or used as target practice by the military. When Henry heard the news, he was noted as saying, 'Well golly gosh gee. I mean, I have worked hard my entire life to earn my money. But I guess kids will be kids. What the hey. I mean, those college kids and minorities need money too right? Asking them to work would be awfully racist of me. I saw a government movie about racism once and they told me it is a terrible thing.' Henry then smiled and returned to his job of grinding aborted fetuses into anti wrinkle cream. A machine could have done his job, but Happy Corp's motto at the time was: Our aborted fetuses are ground to a bloody disgusting pulp by hand so that you can feel that old fashioned, hand made, ground up, human fetus goodness in every putrid rotting ounce you fucking moron. We already know you're going to buy this so who gives a shit? I should apologize, as narrator of this story, not only have I strayed from the subject, but I have been terribly politically incorrect. I meant not to say 'aborted fetuses' but instead 'socially liberated, strong independent fetuses that don't need no womb.' We'll have more on Hillary and her rally today after this commercial break."

The story ended on that tangent as a pile of morbidly obese, nude, Asian men appeared on screen as a preview for that night's episode of Rice Ball Nice Ball. Thomas knew full and well about the Hillary Clinton rally as it was to be held in the clearing outside of his window. Joe was typical of her supporters and Thomas cringed at the thought of her taking power.

"There are just so many more of them then me," he thought. "I have to get out of this place."

He clutched the yellowed paper in his hand.

"Maybe this is my golden ticket," he thought with a smile.

The idea of a golden ticket came to him from a book he once read in secret. Few Americans knew how to read or write. To be accused of literacy was as good as a death sentence. Twelve years earlier, during a particularly cold winter, the American people burned their novels to keep warm. The works of Poe, King, and Hawthorne disappeared from America overnight. Not even the Declaration of Independence escaped the flames. The fact that the mysterious visitor passed a text based message proved to Thomas that something serious was at hand. Thomas turned around on the toilet and lifted his mattress. He reached into a secret compartment in the box spring and retrieved a cache of non-toilet based foods. Precious little non-toilet based foods remained in the ghettos. Fortunately for Thomas, he knew a recluse down the hall who was more than happy to trade the wild vegetables that grew on a pile of corpses outside of his window for Thomas's daily allotment of corn shell cakes, butter chips, corn syrup smoothies, and cigarette pills.

"Hillary, Hillary!" a crowd chanted outside of Thomas's window.

Thomas popped half of an orange into his mouth and chewed it as he walked to his front door. Rapturous applause sounded outside of Thomas's window.

"Must be twelve o'clock," he said as he held the rusty tin doorknob between his hairy fingers.

Thomas looked over his shoulder at the filthy room he had been forced to sleep in for the past half year. Somehow, he knew he would never see it again.

4.

Thomas's old brown shoes shuffled across the peeling linoleum floor. He walked past the man from the next room over and waved. The neighbor was typical of the modern man and recoiled in fear, shrieked "Oh god, don't hurt me!" and scurried back into his apartment to breast-feed from his morbidly obese life partner Pat. Thomas passed three closed doors as he approached the stairwell that led down to the security station between the apartment complex and the street. Thomas put his right hand onto a cold plastic railing and looked back. There, a reclusive neighbor peered at Thomas from a pitch-black doorway.

"Are you leaving?" the man or woman asked.

During Thomas's half year living in the ghetto, he had never once witnessed the recluse leaving its apartment or saw it well enough to determine its gender.

"Looks like it," Thomas replied.

"Could you get me some corn nuggets while you're out? I accidentally flushed mine again," the recluse asked.

"Sure thing," Thomas replied while heading downstairs. "On second thought," he suddenly said while turning back.

Thomas tossed his apartment keys, which landed at the recluse's feet.

"I have seven cans of corn nuggets in a pile between my bed and the wall. If you can bring yourself to leave your room, you're more than welcome to them."

The recluse stared at the keys on the floor and neither moved or replied. As Thomas turned back and walked downstairs, he heard the recluse's door creak shut. The wooden stairwell proved to be as noisy as it was cracked. Groans accompanied every step Thomas took. Thomas meant to take the final step down but took two backwards instead as a wheelchair-bound woman rolled into his path.

"Get the fuck out of my way!" she belched while taking a bite from a perfect cube of cheddar cheese.

"Pardon me miss. I'm not entirely certain how I could have avoided seeing you," Thomas replied while he waited for the woman to roll past him, towards the elevators.

"I said get the fuck out of my way you burnt toast looking piece of shit!" she said while poking Thomas in the chest with her mechanical grabber arm.

Thomas opened his mouth to reply but nothing came out. Behind the screaming woman, a security officer stood before a massive revolving door made of steel reinforced concrete. He was an elderly man, wasted from drink and unable to stand without shaking. He put his liver spotted hand onto the automatic rifle slung over his boney shoulders.

"Just stand to the side kid," He said while smelling his own outstretched index finger.

Thomas obeyed and the wheelchair bound woman slumped forward. Her gelatinous mass stuck to the stairs like a ball of mottled corn syrup.

"Took you long enough," she snarled as she rolled up the stairway.

Her wheelchair caught in the immense bulk of her backside and came along with her. The cufflink on Thomas's right hand caught on the woman's left big toe and tore loose as

Thomas hurried to the security station.

"Almost had to rough you up," the old man said while checking Thomas's ID. "I could have you know. I could shoot you right now. I might like it, might feel good," he said while filling out the necessary forms. "When a man gets my age and his pecker stops working, and his wife gets brittle and dried out, and he tries anal but it makes his shits all watery, and cigarette pills stop working, maybe shooting some people makes him feel real good. You know what I'm saying shit head?" he said while handing Thomas a temporary street pass.

The old man reached over and pressed a shiny red button on the wall. His finger lingered on the button, as though it felt pleasant to touch.

"This is my favorite button," he said dreamily. "It looks just like the candy rations I earn for every five days I go without pistol-whipping a tenant," he continued while rubbing his stomach and licking his mustache.

Thomas stepped forward into the revolving concrete door. On the wall directly in front of his face, he saw an advert for Hillary Clinton's presidential campaign that depicted the woman holding a crucified fetus in one hand and a pistol in the other. The caption below her read, "My religion, my body, my country." A nasally voice emitting from a small speaker located beside a pistol barrel read the caption aloud. As Thomas feigned illiteracy, a powerful tower of daylight struck him, and the road revolved into view.

"You have a nice day now!" the old man said before the door made a complete rotation.

Thomas looked first to his left. There he saw a young Hispanic woman wielding a broom handle like a baseball bat. She tore one of her thirty-seven children from the group and cast her against the sidewalk. The child shrieked and shielded her crown with the soiled paper back novel clutched in her hands.

"Free thought is war and violence against women!" the mother screamed while striking her daughter in the ribs. "What would Hillary think? Women should be independent and free to do exactly as our political leaders instruct us!" she continued as Thomas looked to his right.

There he saw three young Caucasian males discussing how best to spend their government allotted allowances. The fat one suggested they purchase some butter fries. The fatter one suggested they go to the downtown hookertorium and put in applications for the STD section. The fattest of them began to speak, but clutched his chest and fell to the ground in a convulsive fit. His two friends checked him for a pulse. Finding none, or at least feigning to find none, they tore into his flesh with brittle, yellowed teeth. Thomas grimaced as he passed them by. To reach his destination he needed to turn right at the end of the block, walk two blocks further, and turn right into the clearing outside of his bedroom window. People often gave Thomas dirty looks as he walked down the street. Most Americans were either too obese or too lazy to walk. Dozens of persons on motorized wheelchairs pushed past Thomas as they made their way to the Hillary rally. A few of the more adventurous passers by rolled along the ground like humanoid meatballs in a manner similar to the woman on the stairs. A mother and daughter pair rolled past Thomas slowly.

"Look at that loser," the daughter said loudly while slurping up a corn sausage she found on the side of the road.

"Yeah, he must not be drinking his daily recommended dosage of lard," the mother replied.

She finished by spitting at Thomas's right shoe, but

missed and struck a wheel chair bound person on the left most big toe instead. The viscous nature of her spittle caused it to act as a stinking yellow rope and she pulled away from her daughter at an amazing speed. The powered wheelchair took a sharp right turn, causing the mother to swing hard left into a stack of garbage bags. She looked as though about to weep; until she realized she landed atop a puddle of half-eaten pork cakes someone had recently vomited onto the side of the road. She then smiled and began to feast. Thomas frowned as he turned the corner. The cracked pavement glistened with red white and blue light reflected from the backs of the uncountable wheelchairs headed towards the Hillary Clinton rally. Thomas hurried down the final two blocks. That area of the ghetto was notorious as the stomping grounds of the local gang of repressed homosexuals and Thomas did not intend to cross them. Three members of the gang sat atop a stoop outside of their building's rotating door. They sat side by side with their hands in the back pockets of each-others skinny jeans. One of them coughed as Thomas walked by. Thomas looked over. His hazel eyes met the dark brown eyes of the repressed homosexual in the middle.

"Why are you looking at me like I'm some kind of faggot, you queer?" the middle-most repressed homosexual called out to Thomas.

Thomas meant to continue walking but felt frozen in place.

"I ain't never sucked a dick that one time. Not never! Screw you pal, you're lucky I don't kick your stupid, perfectly-rounded, and cuddly ass!" the middle-most repressed homosexual continued.

"You tell him honey buns," the left-most, not nearly as repressed homosexual on the stoop added while man-queefing into the middle-most repressed homosexual's palm.

As the middle-most repressed homosexual retracted his hand and smelled it, a trickle of spunk seeped between the rhinestones bedazzled onto his crotch. Thomas shook his head and walked away. Plain cubed buildings cast shadows across Thomas's shoulders, reminding him of the limitations of the ghetto. Cold grey walls obscured ignorant and lazy citizens. Thomas thought of all the persons around him that thought of nothing, produced nothing, and cared for nothing.

"Why do they even live?" he wondered as he watched a legless Asian man drive past on a rickshaw pulled by his two rolling children.

The Asian smiled as he passed Thomas and called out, "Like twin Buddhas, aren't they? Good thing I only drowned their sisters!"

References to religion were not uncommon in America. However, Thomas was slightly taken aback to hear someone mention one of the old world religions. There were plenty of new, government approved, religions to turn to after all. In fact, the government mandated at least one religion per person. Thomas however, found none that suited his needs. There were the Christericans, who believed Jesus was a really cool guy that wanted you to join the army. There were the Neo Jews that were just like the old Jews, but slightly jewier. There were no Muslims left in America, of course. They had not been harassed or deported, but left of their own volition upon finding rendered pig fat in the drinking water. There were at least fifty other government approved religious denominations to choose from. Thomas always told people he was a Lard Colaian. According to their entertainment cube adds, they believed that Lard Cola was "The best cola ever and that you should totally break into Henry Shackleford's house, steal something, sell it for allowance credits, buy some Lard Cola, and drink it to the extreme!" Thomas chose the religion due to their lack of a mandatory weekly meeting and the free case of Lard Cola he received once a month.

Thomas turned the final corner. There, in the open area beneath his window, he saw a multitude of sweaty, glistening American bodies that resembled wheelchair bound sausages rotting in the sun. The road he tread gradually declined towards the temporary plastic podium where Hillary would make her speech. Thomas grinned and imagined shoving one wheelchair forward, causing a domino effect that would knock over every heaving pile of humanoid disappointment in his path. It was not that Thomas hated fat people. He did not hate anyone based on religion, race, appearance, political affiliations, or creed. Two long years of mandatory mental reprogramming trained him to think that way. In fact, if anything, he was conditioned to hate himself for harboring free thought and self-reliance. Thomas thought back to his two years of torture and education. He wanted to think back further, but something blocked his mind. Without realizing it, Thomas walked right up to the edge of the speaking podium.

A tall, cock eyed Hawaiian in a suit held out his hand and said, "Stop fool. I said to you stop. Fool!"

Thomas looked up, realized where he was, and apologized.

"No, not you cutie pie, I meant the slag to your left,' the bodyguard replied while winking his crooked eye.

Thomas looked to his left as a five-foot six-inch tall, tan, red-head walked away with tears streaming down her lovely freckled face and onto her well filled out turquoise dress. Thomas meant to run after her, but the body guard held him in place. Over his shoulder, Hillary Clinton stood atop a large white plastic slab and cleared her throat as she approached a plastic podium. A Caucasian male, his Caucasian mother, his Caucasian wife, and his government appointed black daughter stood ten feet behind and to the left of Hillary. The speaking slab was five feet off the ground so all in attendance could see them well. They were a well dressed family and the government appointed black daughter very well behaved despite only being a six year old future diversity hire. Hillary tapped the non-phallic, woman-approved, microphone with her yellowed index finger. Hillary was an extraordinarily beautiful woman by the current American standard. She was able to stand under her own power so long as someone held her by the elbow, look down, see her open toed leather sandals, and touch her hands together in the front as well as the back. Her bleached blonde hair fell onto the exquisite four-inch thick shoulder pads of her business suit. Her hips tapered down, showing only a hint of her self-empowerment, penile simulation codpiece. Something metallic gleamed from her breast pocket. Thomas raised his hand to block the glint as Hillary began to speak.

"Oh I see we have a volunteer already!" she said with a grin.

Hillary's mouth seemed stretched and cadaverous. Thomas looked around, and realized all eyes, save for the body guard's one lazy eye, were set upon him. Before he could react, the bodyguard grabbed Thomas by the buttock cheeks, smelled his hair, and thrust him onto the stage. Thomas blinked several times; uncertain of what had happened as Hillary continued to speak.

"Free thought is war. The government knows who you are and what you need!"

The crowd burst into rapturous applause but quickly petered out as their arms grew too tired to continue. Hillary paused for a moment while those in attendance took a swig from their corn sauce, Lard Colas, and diet butter shakes.

"All war is war on women. We are the first to suffer in

war," she continued as the man, his mother, his wife, and his government appointed black daughter stepped forward. "We lose our husbands, our sons, our brothers, our fathers, and our platonic male friends that we use for attention and free dinners," Hillary said while making an overly animated sad expression. "You see," Hillary continued while pulling a pistol from her pocket. "If I was to kill this man right now, he wouldn't suffer, his family would, maybe even the chocolate bunny too."

Thomas reached out to pull Hillary's arm aside, but acted one third of a second too late. Artificial thunder shot through the air like the initial spark of an immense flame. Thomas stumbled past Hillary and stood over the crumpled body of the murdered American man. His wife and mother held each other and soaked their shoulder pads in tears. The black daughter poked the corpse with her foot and said "Eh."

"Do you see?" Hillary asked with great, feigned emotion. "Free thought is war! These women are suffering needlessly due to war!" she yelled over an outburst of orgasmic applause.

She leveled her pistol at the back of Thomas's head. He felt the cold touch of metal between his bristly hairs.

"And you, are you a free thinker?" Hillary asked in a low, emotionless voice.

Thomas swallowed hot phlegm that stuck in the base of his throat and imagined his life ending to rapturous applause. As Thomas turned back, Hillary jammed the pistol into his left eye socket.

"Properly trained dogs don't turn to face an angry master," Hillary whispered while pressing her finger against the trigger.

The audience fell silent save for a few dozen outbursts of

flatulence. Thomas grabbed the pistol slowly and attempted to push it away. Hillary held it in place with an iron grip and smiled. Thomas panicked, breathing in and out three times in rapid succession as he fought the urge to vomit. Upon the final heave, the phlegm lodged in his throat broke loose and struck Hillary in the eyes. Thomas then grabbed the pistol and threw it into the crowd as Hillary recoiled.

"Quickly, this way!" a familiar voice called from the backside of the stage.

Thomas followed the voice and ran past the grieving mother and bride, as well as the indifferent government appointed black child. As Thomas dropped over the side of the stage, a tall man in a black suit and wide brimmed hat ran towards a distant, idling van. Thomas recognized him as the interloper from the Approved Speech Hour and doubted that he headed towards a trap. All enclosed vehicles had been banned in order to facilitate the sales of government approved, lard powered wheelchairs two years earlier. Only a fellow free thinker would utilize such a vehicle. The stranger struggled to get into the drivers seat. Something about his right foot prevented him from sliding in easily. As Thomas sprinted, a mass of rolling, obese bodies chased after him.

"Break his commie legs!" a man screamed from the back of the pack.

"We'll drown him in butter and eat him alive!" a four hundred pound four year old girl squealed from the middle.

At the head of the pack, Joe stood atop a motorized wheelchair, his frilly dress sparkling brilliantly beneath the neon sky.

"Stop that man, pu-lease! He and I need to talk about our relationship!" he screamed in a shrill, falsetto voice.

He came to a stop as Thomas clambered onto the passenger seat of the van.

"What do we do now you fat fruiting bombaclot?" a mildly morbidly obese Jamaican woman asked as she rolled to a stop.

"We miss him," Joe whispered as the van pulled away.

A single tear fell from the false eyelashes of his left eye and landed on the tip of his shit encrusted penis.

5.

Cold puffs of breath fogged the interior of the van. Balled up millipedes rolled across the rusted sheet-metal floor. As Thomas pulled his seat-belt over his shoulder, he found the fabric torn and the buckle end useless.

"Did you dredge this thing out of a landfill or something?" Thomas asked as he looked to his left and studied the features of his supposed savior.

The stranger was about Thomas's age, but worn worse from his years. Tiny scratches marked the skin around his sunken eyes. Curly black hair fell in odd trestles around his filthy ears and merged with his graying beard. The black wide brimmed hat on his head was caked with sweat and looked as though it had never been removed. His black suit looked threadbare and in desperate need of mending. The driver noticed Thomas's gaze and spoke.

"My name is Kuzen, and yes, I did get this from a dump."

Kuzen took a sharp right turn. The right side wheels of the van lifted slightly. Garbage bags, backed up sewage, and sleeping politicians lined most Ghetto streets; making the road narrow and perilous for an old-fashioned vehicle to traverse.

"Why did you help me?" Thomas asked.

Kuzen cleared his throat and spat out of his window. His spittle flew through the air and struck a round sign with an image depicting a red white and blue cheeseburger on one side and a depiction of Jesus kneeling before the American flag on the other.

"You got my letter didn't you?" Kuzen replied. "I wanted to talk some things over but you climbed right up on stage and made a mess of things."

Thomas nodded and felt for the letter in his pocket. He found nothing and realized that he had dropped it during his escape.

"Why me?" Thomas asked. "And what for?" he added after Kuzen neglected to reply.

The van passed through a haze of yellow smoke. Thomas and Kuzen rolled up their windows.

"I have an offer for you," Kuzen said while slowing the van to a stop.

They parked at the edge of the ghetto. Most populated areas existed within a boundary of concrete barriers and knee-high walls. Since most Americans could not walk, let alone climb a knee-high wall, very few persons escaped into the intermediate areas. Yellow smoke clogged the street, but through the break in the barrier, Thomas saw green grass swaying in the breeze.

"You want me to go with you somewhere, outside of the ghetto. Is that it?" Thomas asked.

Kuzen nodded and opened his door. He stepped outside and pulled his jacket collar over his mouth.

"What is that god awful stench?" he asked.

"It's a gaseous form of butter," Thomas replied. "They pump it into the air to calm the locals whenever something goes awry."

Kuzen reached behind his seat and retrieved a musty, navy-blue gym bag. He then turned and walked towards the concrete barrier at the edge of the ghetto. Neon lights shimmered across the gap between the artificial sky and the knee high walls. Yellow sunlight bled through that gap, onto Thomas's feet. They stood in silence for a moment, then squeezed between the gap.

Once Thomas made it through, he remarked, "The average American could never squeeze through that opening."

"We aren't average Americans," Kuzen replied. He pushed the brim of his hat up slightly and added, "We aren't even Americans at all."

Thomas meant to ask for clarification, but became awestruck by what he saw outside of the city. Pristine white clouds darted through the sapphire colored sky. In the ghetto, electronic product placements and government slogans blotted out the sun and stars alike. After two years of reprogramming, Thomas had come to think of his blurred memories of the sky as a delusional dream. A red robin landed at Thomas's feet. It pecked at some dried corn shells that stuck to the toe of his right shoe. Thomas studied the bird for a moment and smiled. The bird then turned around and shat on Thomas's shoe.

"What do you mean, we aren't Americans?" Thomas asked while punting the bird.

Kuzen walked towards a three-foot tall black drop cloth covered item in the distance and screamed, "Follow if you want to know!" as he broke into an awkward sprint.

As Thomas hurried to catch up, he realized that Kuzen had two left feet. Thomas hunched over to catch his breath. Kuzen tore the drop cloth free and flung it into the air, revealing two aluminum bikes.

"Get on," Kuzen said while mounting one of the bikes.

Thomas followed suit and had little trouble keeping pace with Kuzen despite Kuzen's longer legs.

"Are you ok riding that thing?" Thomas asked.

One of Kuzen's legs pumped normally while the other jostled side to side.

"I lost my right leg from the knee down during the Great Change of Power, not that you'd know much about that. There's a seven year waiting list for right leg prosthetics so I've had to make due," Kuzen said while pulling ahead.

They passed a rain-slicked tent where a young mother, her husband, and their child sat around a dying fire. Only the child noticed Kuzen and Thomas. She held up her little hand and waved. Both Kuzen and Thomas replied in kind.

"There are free people outside of the ghettos?" Thomas asked.

"Are you going to miss this place, New Something or other?" Kuzen asked as though not hearing Thomas's question.

"I don't know," Thomas replied. "It used to be New Something. But that something it was, is long gone now. Now it's not even Old Something anymore; just another cube of grey buildings in a cube of grey ghettos."

They traveled the next fifteen minutes in silence. On the sixteenth minute, they reached the peak of a sharp drop and the ocean came into view. A sudden recollection burst in Thomas's mind like an old-fashioned Christmas light that burns down the tree, the house, and family sleeping in their beds. Thomas saw his legs dangling from his father's knee. His mother and a young boy waded knee deep in champagne colored waves. Somehow, it seemed as though they were standing before that same ocean, but from the opposite side. How long it had been since Thomas thought of his family, he could not recall. Where they had gone in the last two and a half years, or if they were even alive, he had no idea. Kuzen jumped from his bike and watched it roll downhill and into the sea. He then hobbled downhill and shot a flare across the inky water. A response flare exploded crimson in the sky, Illuminating the last patch of long grass separating the hill from the sea,

"Did you enjoy our little ride through the country?" Kuzen asked as a medium sized passenger boat hurried towards them.

It was an ancient vessel with rotten wooden planks and a partially collapsed cabin in the center. A large person, likely the captain, stood in an outhouse-sized compartment at the front of the boat and steered it towards the shore.

"It was relaxing," Thomas replied after a brief pause.

"I'm glad to hear that," Kuzen said.

As the boat pulled ashore, murky water washed over Thomas and Kuzen's shoes.

"Because this is the last peaceful stretch of land we'll see until we reach Ungland," Kuzen said as he clambered over the side of the boat.

Thomas did not know what to make of his new friend's warning and he had no idea what Ungland was either. As he contemplated his circumstances, a massive woman with leathery, sun-stained skin reached over the edge of the boat and grabbed Thomas by the shoulder. Filthy pubic hairs and mottled smegma lined the creases of her wrinkled hands.

"Welcome aboard the Salted Clam," she said with a

steaming belch. "It's bad luck to start a voyage without a kiss," she added as she pulled Thomas aboard with a jerking motion and jammed her hot, phlegm flavored tongue down his throat.

The dark brown hairs on her lips tickled Thomas so terribly that he stiff-armed the woman in the face. He felt what he assumed were hairy moles beneath his fingers. Some of them fell off and crawled across his arm.

"This is all quite unnecessary," Thomas said with as much dignity as he could muster.

"Don't be so modest. After all, it's my body and my choice," the woman replied with a crooked yellow grin.

As she stepped forward and winked at Thomas, a pubic louse crawled from one of her wrinkled brown forehead folds and disappeared into a blackhead on the bridge of her nose. Her freakishly small hands reached into Thomas pockets. With one hand, she stole a roll a breath mints. With the other, she grasped Thomas's penis and gave him a little pinch. Thomas tried to pull away, but the tan woman laughed and shoved him backwards over Kuzen's gym bag. Thomas fell and cracked his head on the gunwale. In dreams, Thomas sat outside a home he could not quite remember. A man he assumed to be his father bounced him on his knee while the woman he assumed was his mother read him a story. Her words were garbled and impossible to discern. Thomas looked to his left in his dream and saw the little boy from his memory of the ocean. He held a penknife in his hand and thrust it into Thomas's stomach. Feeling the pain as though it were real, Thomas awoke from his dream. He sat up on his wooden bunk and pulled up his shirt. There, in the dim light of the boat's interior, he ran his left index finger across a needlepoint scar that he had noticed before, but previously paid little mind.

"Have a bad dream?" Kuzen asked.

He sat on a bunk on the other side of the room and polished his boots with the corner of his blanket.

"You've been out for a while," he added as Thomas grasped his aching head.

"Where the hell are you taking me?" Thomas asked.

"We're going home."

Three other men sat up in their bunks. They were sickly looking men in their late forties. Each bore horrific scars and faded tattoos on their sun-scorched skin.

"You homos talking about your wedding?" one of them asked.

"Going to adopt a little blind Chinese boy and cut off his willy?" another of them interjected.

"I do say, the two of you are being rather uncivilized and blatantly one-dimensional," the third added.

The first two sailors gave him a dirty look. He cleared his throat and continued.

"Actually, I meant to say that you two gentleman are gay lords that like men's buttocks and the smell of feces and ingesting ingots of icky sticky dick drips betwixt your lower affixed buttock lips while talking about how much you prefer the pungent aroma of balls to that of a moist and slippery vagina."

He looked towards his companions, who reacted with raised thumbs and nods of approval.

"These queers don't like pussy the way we do! Hey mate,

tell these faggots how much we love pussy!" one of the less well spoken sailors cried.

"Why, my good sirs," the well spoken sailor began, "This man here is so straight that if my hairy, disgusting, supple man ass was a woman's vagina he'd make sweet love to it this very instant."

"Which I do every Saturday night, mind you, because I'm just that straight!" the third sailor interjected.

"Never mind these morons," Kuzen said to Thomas. "They've been drinking salt water again."

"No I haven't!" one of them objected before looking into the cup clenched in his hand. He then added, "Oh wait, I have!" before falling to the cabin floor in a convulsive fit.

The second sailor spat out his drink and threw the cup to the floor.

"I do say. I believe my entire existence may be a hallucination," the third sailor added.

He put his hands to his face and began to scream before immediately fading out of existence. The two remaining sailors clung together and trembled violently. Kuzen stood and walked towards the doorway. He gestured for Thomas to follow, but a barrel-chested woman in a blood red coat blocked their path.

"There's been a change of plans," she announced in a deep, gravelly voice. "The damned idiot crew's been drinking salt water again and we'll have to pull into port in England."

"Isn't that where we were heading?" Thomas asked.

Kuzen shook his head without turning around.

"You shouldn't interrupt the captain like that. She's got so much sand in her cunt she queefs pearls," Kuzen whispered ominously.

The large woman fixed her yellow eyes on Thomas. Kuzen took a step to the left but the woman easily shoved him aside.

"My last name is Neater. My friends call me Tampo," The captain said.

"Hello Tampo," Thomas replied.

The captain grasped Thomas's brown lapels with meaty, patchouli-scented hands.

"Listen here pretty boy. I don't like you. I don't like your fancy five-dollar haircut, I hate your upright posture, and I don't want you touching my precious salted clam!" she screamed while lifting Thomas an inch off the ground.

"Your precious salted clam?" Thomas asked bewilderedly.

He looked over the captain's shoulder. There he perceived the filthy hag that kissed him, peering through the doorway.

"I didn't mean any disrespect miss," Thomas began to say.

Tampo lifted him another inch into the air and his head struck the cabin roof.

"Sir, I mean! I meant to say sir," Thomas quickly said.

The captain's mannish arms felt like concrete against Thomas's ribs. The pubic lice crawling through her buzz cut jumped onto Thomas's crotch and began to eat through his trousers.

"You're a very masculine person and I'm certain that your um, lovely girlfriend thinks I'm an insignificant spec of a man compared to you. I'm most certain your clitoris is gigantic and worthy of envy, even from men," he added, trying to sound as sincere as possible.

The Salted Clam lurched forward violently, knocking Kuzen and the hag to the floor. Only the captain and her captive remained stationary. The hag tried to grasp Kuzen's backside but he donkey kicked her in the face and scrambled to his feet.

"You're lucky I have a ship to steer, you, you hag fag!" the captain said while dropping Thomas to the ground. "When we reach land, you and I are going to have a very hot, moist, and sweaty conversation," she added while backing up to the doorway. She put her arm around the hag's shoulder as she stood and added, "You'll feel the full body of my message. For your sake I hope you're a cunning linguist."

Dry bile rose in the back of Thomas's throat. The captain smirked and blew him a toothy kiss before walking away with her hag. Tampo's rancid, sour milk flavored breath, struck Thomas square in the face. He struggled to hold back his breakfast as he hurriedly scraped the parasites from his clothing.

"Think she'd make a good girlfriend?" Thomas asked sheepishly when he noticed Kuzen's eyes upon him.

"I think you almost became Tampo's girlfriend," Kuzen replied.

Thomas stood and adjusted his shirt collar.

"Are you ready to tell me what this is all about?" he asked as they stepped onto the deck.

Kuzen placed his hands against the gunwale and felt ancient white paint crumble beneath his shaking fingers.

"I meant to tell you everything in Ungland."

"You mean England right?"

"No. And now that we have to stop in England, that will mean either waiting there for two weeks while the captain prepares a new crew for the trip to Ungland, or spending several days walking to Ungland across several nations' borders."

A seagull swooped down and hovered over Kuzen's shoulder. He felt the air displaced by its flapping wings and removed his wide brimmed hat, revealing his thinning black hair. The gull then veered to the left and plopped a hot searing shit onto the bridge of Kuzen's bony nose. Thomas took three steps back and fought the urge to laugh. Kuzen wiped his eyes with a cloth he produced from his interior coat pocket and spat over the side of the boat.

"I'll tell you what's up once we dock in England," Kuzen announced. "Then we'll decide how best to travel home."

"Back to America?"

Kuzen shook his head side to side and pointed to a small mass of land in the distance. Cold ocean spray covered them in a fine silvery mist. Kuzen replaced his hat atop his head and turned to face Thomas.

"We'll reach England come nightfall. Keep your hands in

your pockets and your wits about you. Though the Brits aren't in the same boat as the Americans, they have their own share of troubles. Follow my lead and we'll do fine. Panic and we'll be lucky to survive."

Thomas looked away from Kuzen and contemplated the word 'survive'. After all, was that not all he had done for the past two and a half years? Thomas grit his teeth and came to a decision. No matter what Kuzen meant to propose, Thomas would accept. Surviving was no longer enough. Thomas intended to live. Clattering footsteps approached suddenly. A tattooed sailor ran between Thomas and Kuzen, vomiting over the side of the gunwale so hard that his feet lifted from the splintered deck. After a tremendous wave struck the Salted Clam, that sailor tumbled overboard, and Thomas watched him sink in silence.

6.

The Salted Clam lurched forward as the motors switched off. Kuzen retrieved a small glass jar from his navy-blue gym bag. A large, luminescent moth clung to the glass. The eye shaped markings on its wings seemed to stare at Thomas. Kuzen smiled as he shook the jar, then rolled it into the cabin. Dim blue lights flickered from within.

"Tampo plans to ride out the current the rest of the way in. But you and I have other plans," he whispered as he clambered over the gunwale.

Thomas looked over his shoulder at the captain's compartment. Tampo leaned against the outer wall of her quarters and licked the lesions on the back of the ship hag's neck. One broke off against the captain's tongue and she bit into it like a rancid orange slice. The hag looked back at Thomas and smirked. Thomas stumbled backwards and fell overboard. Moonlight rippled on the surface of the water like a silver ring.

"Are we sneaking in so the locals won't catch us?" Thomas asked after righting himself in the water.

"Nope," Kuzen replied.

He smiled from ear to ear and hurried towards the shore. Blue luminescence grew from the stern of the Salted Clam. A hard wind blew and the glow grew into a mighty wall of amber flames. Alarms blared from the shoreline. Three motorboats launched from a distant port and headed for the Salted Clam.

"Is that the fire patrol?" Thomas asked.

"No, that was the police. No one is allowed to enter or leave England without the Queen's consent."

"Will Tampo be alright?"

"Right now, I'm more worried about finding a place to sleep," Kuzen replied as he stepped onto English sand.

After ringing out their clothes, they crept across the beach and into a bustling city with enough lit windows to challenge the supremacy of the stars. Thomas was so awestruck that he did not notice the person who approached from the sea. That person stood on the shore, tore a lamprey from their chest, and jammed it down the back of their pants.

"See something special?" Kuzen asked.

"There's not one grey cube of a building." Thomas replied.

Failing to obscure a smile, Kuzen stepped forward instead and stumbled on a small metallic object. A small camera mounted atop remote controlled vehicle focused its lens on Kuzen. Luckily, a woman in a short skirt walked by and it sped off to follow her.

"What the hell was that?" Thomas asked.

"Nothing is private in England," Kuzen replied in a hushed voice. "Japs visiting Pearl Harbor take less pictures."

Thomas meant to inquire further, but a woman caught his eye. Her flaxen hair fell upon milky white shoulders. She noticed Thomas, and smiled. A crust of bread hung from her ceiling-beam-sized teeth.

"You look lost. Can I help you with something?" she asked.

As she spoke, her front-most teeth cut into and chewed a

portion of Thomas's shoulder.

"That's ok," Thomas said while trying to hide his horror. "I'm looking for a place to stay for the night, but I can see that you're busy."

"You're welcome to spend the night with me," She said while batting her beautiful eyes. "Your friend could even bunk with my mother."

A little old lady approached. Kuzen meant to pull Thomas away, but a police officer loomed nearby and he decided to act casual instead.

"I'm very close to my mother. You see, my father abandoned me as a child," the woman continued.

She intended to say more, but the police man intervened. He cracked the woman's mother across the crown with a strange, semi transparent billy-club, then put her into a sophisticated head lock.

"What is the meaning of this?" the younger woman screamed.

Wall mounted cameras swiveled towards her. Thomas and Kuzen did their best to casually obscure their faces.

The police officer cleared his throat while sneering at the woman, then replied, "You pathetic result of buggery. Isn't it obvious? If your father abandoned you as a child, he must have conceived you when he was a child! By comparing your age with your mothers, I must conclude that this disgusting creature is in fact, a pedophile!"

The officer tightened his hold and began to carry the mother away.

The daughter attempted to protest, but the officer cut her off saying, "Madam, with the exception of the royal family and certain members of the BBC upper management, passionate, sweaty, unforgettably awkward intercourse with children is illegal in this country!"

As the officer carried his prisoner away, Thomas and Kuzen darted between wandering couples until they reached a fork in the road. They found a bakery to the left. To the right, they noticed a gathering of strangely dressed men and women.

"What's with the weird scarves on their faces?" Thomas asked as one of the men turned towards him.

"This road is a Scotsria Law Zone, filled with Scottish Muslims who toss acid from bags of haggis and force their women to wear kilts on their faces," Kuzen replied.

"Really?" Thomas asked.

"Don't be silly, we're actually dyslexic crossdressers!" one of those oddly dressed persons replied.

Kuzen shrugged and headed towards the bakery. Were Thomas and Kuzen listening, they would have heard the click clack of high heels following them the entire way.

Crumbs and discarded tea bags littered the grey tiled floor of the bakery. Salt air poured in through a small rectangular window on each wall, save for the one to the right of Thomas's chosen table. There, the baker and his wife stood behind a knee-high counter, rolling bread and counting the days take. Kuzen approached them before joining Thomas at his table.

"We'll take two bowls of whatever is still hot at this

hour."

The baker looked up from his dough and nodded. Kuzen placed some coins on the counter and joined Thomas at his table. He meant to put up his legs, but Thomas pointed towards the counter. There Kuzen saw the displeased gaze of the baker's wife. He smiled sheepishly and set his legs back onto the floor.

"Wouldn't want to piss her off. You've seen the mural haven't you?" Kuzen asked while pointing towards the brim of his hat.

Thomas casually peered over Kuzen's head. The bakery ceiling bore an elaborate mural of the baker, his wife, and their four sons beating up a group of Irish children. The mural depicted the owner biting a little girl on the arm and his sons tearing out tufts of her orange hair. The baker's wife was depicted performing an impressive spinning kick, with each leg striking a different Irish child in the ribs. Thomas would have made a remark, but the sound of clattering plates stayed his tongue. The baker's wife set a basket of bread, an empty teacup, and a bowl of murky grey soup in front of either patron. She then placed a butter knife and a stick of butter in the center of the table.

"We didn't order any tea," Kuzen said when he saw the baker's wife reaching for the teapot on the counter.

"It's complimentary," She said with a grin.

"Well, I've never rebuked a complement from a lady," Kuzen replied.

The baker's wife poured Kuzen a cup as a flying camera flew over her shoulder.

"Looks like you have a fan in the monitoring

department," Thomas said.

"I have many fans," the baker's wife replied. "And there's nothing a bakers husband loves more than chowing down on a freshly baked cream pie," she said with a wink.

Thomas did not understand. Kuzen smiled and made a mental note to return to the bakery after finding Thomas somewhere safe to sleep. Thomas and Kuzen tore into their soup. It was slightly acrid, with a bitter aftertaste, but ultimately satisfying. Thomas reached for the butter knife to load up a roll. Noticing a cork stuck to the end of the knife, Thomas furrowed his brow and attempted to pry it loose. After three hard tugs, the cork went flying, and the hand that held the knife shot upwards.

The baker and his wife stood from their chairs behind the counter and recoiled in fear.

"This man is brandishing a knife!" the baker screamed.

Thomas and Kuzen looked at each other in confusion. Before they could react, the baker ran past their table and blocked the entrance with his body. The baker's wife kicked Thomas in the stomach and performed a spinning kick directly to Kuzen's left testicle. Fortunately, his other testicle cushioned the blow. Sirens blared outside.

"We can't afford to get caught!" Kuzen screeched.

He stood, shoved the baker's wife aside, and pushed Thomas towards an open window. Thomas stood upon a table and scrambled outside.

"Meet me where we dried off!" Kuzen called.

He intended to follow Thomas out the window, but the Bakers wife kicked at Kuzen and would have caved in his chest if the blow had landed. He scrambled backwards and jumped through the window on the opposite wall. Cold wind blew against his beard as the baker and his wife caught Kuzen by the legs. The husband pulled on Kuzen's natural left leg. The baker's wife pulled on his prosthetic second left leg.

"I thought we had something going on back there," Kuzen cried as he struggled to kick his way free.

"I preferred the other guy!" the baker replied.

"Not you!" Kuzen screamed.

"I'll visit you in prison!" the baker's wife added.

Police officers in fuzzy black hats ran towards Kuzen from an adjacent alley. He reached back and undid the bolt that kept his prosthetic leg in place. Then lurched forward and fell from the window. His left arm landed on a rake that shot up and struck him in the ribs. His black hat floated down and landed on his stomach. Kuzen looked back, hoping his prosthetic leg would follow. The sound of approaching boots brought Kuzen to his senses. He grabbed the rake and jammed it under his right arm as a make-shift crutch, then replaced his hat atop his bald spot and hobbled towards the shore.

Thomas sprinted through the winding dirt and cobble stone streets. He meant to retreat to the shore, but flying cameras blocked his path. As Thomas swatted them down, he completely lost his way. Police officers in fuzzy black hats pursued Thomas and kept a respectable pace. Thomas pushed through the crowds and sprinted until he could run no more. He hunched over panting at the foot of a colossal clock tower. It was certainly not the famous Big Ben tower. No, that relic was lost during the Great Change of Power. Thomas looked up and read a silver placard at the base of the tower. He found that he was hunched over in the shadow of "Not Nearly Big Enough to be

Considered Big in the Traditional Sense of the Word but Certainly Large Enough to Warrant our Admiration and Respect in these Modern Times Ben." Three policemen stood fifteen feet away and closed in on Thomas slowly. Thomas was too tired to flee or to care if they caught him. The first police officer to approach Thomas was a tall, sinewy man. Every muscle in his face was visible, and when he smiled at Thomas, his face resembled an over cooked turkey stuffed with piano keys.

"Oy, what's all this then?" the officer asked while pulling a pink balloon from a holster on his left hip.

He took two deep breaths to inflate the elongated balloon and brandished it in Thomas's direction.

"Is that supposed to be a billy-club?" Thomas asked.

"Now now yankee doodle, there's no cause for alarm. We Brits don't believe in such silly things as weapons, using force, defending ourselves from criminals, dental floss, limiting immigration, or bathing. You just play nice and I'll get you a nice, soft cheeseburger. You'd like that wouldn't you?"

Two years of reprogramming camp still held sway in the back of Thomas's mind.

Thomas's eyes rolled back slightly and he thought to himself, "Yeah, a cheeseburger and a nice Lard Cola would hit the spot."

He began to stick out his hands for cuffs. Fortunately for Thomas, "Not Nearly Big Enough to be Considered Big in the Traditional Sense of the Word but Certainly Large Enough to Warrant our Admiration and Respect in these Modern Times Ben" struck midnight. Its not nearly so big but certainly large enough to warrant our admiration and respect in these modern times sized ring broke Thomas from his stupor. He sprinted away as everyone else stopped to have a cup of tea.

"Kuzen!" Thomas cried as he sprinted.

He pushed past two old men in dresses that sipped tea from a pair of scuffed high-healed shoes. He then turned the corner and the ocean came into view. Thomas ran along the beach calling Kuzen's name but received no reply. He stumbled upon a ten by ten foot shack composed of driftwood on the underside of a tall bluff. A blue and white flag served as the roof. Cold seawater lapped at its exterior walls. Thomas doubted the building's integrity. However, he had a pounding headache and a desperate need for sleep. Thomas kicked the wet sand from his soggy brown shoes and cracked open the door. Pale light poured inside, illuminating all but the furthest corner of the shack. The shack was empty as far as Thomas could see, save for a torn up newspaper in the middle of the room. Thomas stepped forward, intending to make the torn papers his bed.

"Stop right there you filthy land grabbing goy!" someone said.

A shriveled man with protruding ribs stood and pressed the business end of a rifle into Thomas's stomach. The man was practically naked save for a gray cloth slung around his waist and a leather cap stuck to the curly black hairs on the crown of his head.

"I'll just be leaving then," Thomas said while stepping back towards the door.

"Oh no you don't!" the partially nude man screamed.

He lunged forward, took Thomas by the shoulder, and flung him to the ground.

"I'm tired of you filthy gentiles coming on to my sacred Israeli land and polluting it with your filthy goy skin flakes, intact foreskin, and leavened bread!" the mostly nude man screamed.

"Israeli land? I thought I was in England," Thomas said.

He held his throbbing head and tried to look for some means of escape.

"Oh no," the Israeli began. "I have traversed mountain and sea. I have planted my flag on this ten by ten foot patch of land. It is my holy right, my destiny, the natural expansion of my peoples! How dare you tread upon this holiest of ground?" he continued as beads of hot brown ass sweat ran down the back of his spindly legs.

A fine mist of processed sea vapor and phlegm escaped from his sizable nose with every angry breath he drew.

"Really, I meant no disrespect sir. I had no idea that this was holy land," Thomas said as he backed into the darkest corner of the room.

His flailing feet sent torn pages of the discarded newspaper into the air. The Israeli man caught one of the floating papers in his hand and held it to Thomas's face.

"Do you see this, this filth?" he asked with a shaking voice.

It was too dark for Thomas to read, and he was too confused to respond. The Israeli man let his rifle go limp and its metallic tip stuck against Thomas's left thigh.

"This filth was written by an English woman. I liberated some of her land for my people and she had the nerve to accuse me of theft and murder, just because I burned down her home and blew up her children while my relatives watched from a distance and ate popcorn. You goyim are all the same!" he said while leveling the rifle at Thomas's head.

"Maybe she didn't mean it! Maybe it's just satire!"

"Don't talk down to me you filthy foreskin having piece of shit," the Israeli replied. "I know what satire is. Only a complete moron would get this upset over satire!" he screamed while reaching into his rag pants, retrieving a handful of precut foreskins and popping them into his mouth for a quick late night snack.

"I guess you're right. Only a real moron can't tell the difference between satire and hate speech," Thomas interjected.

His good nature got the better of him and he inadvertently smiled.

"Don't laugh at me," the Israeli man said while sliding the bolt of his rifle into place. "When gentiles laugh at me, I become much less than gentle myself. If you know what I mean."

Thomas looked up at the Israeli man for a moment in disbelief. A loud boom sounded and the Israeli fell to the floor. Kuzen stood over Thomas with a broken rake in his hand.

"Who says Jews write the best jokes?" he asked with a grin.

Thomas sprung up and nearly hugged Kuzen before thinking better of it and taking a step backward instead.

"Thank God we're both safe," Thomas said.

"That's not exactly the case," Kuzen replied.

Red and blue lights flashed across the beach. Fifteen policemen, five policewomen, and three men in dresses surrounded the building. Thomas eyed the Israeli's rifle, but Kuzen kicked it away. They submitted to arrest without further resistance. The drive to their holding cell was brief, with only a minor stop for the driver's one a.m. tea. Thomas had questions for Kuzen, but both men passed out on their cots immediately upon entering their cell.

"Bloody yanks. Should ave ad their tea," the officer guarding the door said to someone who stood in shadows.

"Well spoken," that person replied.

7.

Thomas awoke to the soft thuds of plastic striking metal. Kuzen held his right thigh between the open door of the cell while a guard reattached Kuzen's prosthetic leg with a red plastic hammer.

"Don't you have any real tools to work with?" Kuzen asked.

"Our beloved Queen is against anything that could be used for self-defense. I mean, if someone in charge thought about it, they wouldn't even give you back this leg. It's easy to detach and has enough heft to brain a man's eyes back into place," the guard replied.

He kept one crooked eye fixed upon the bolt while the other stared off into space. Every other hammer blow struck off center or missed the bolt entirely. While the guard slowly made progress, Kuzen inspected the condition of his prosthetic. It was composed of an iron rod connected via a hinge to a metallic foot on one end and a sturdy bolt connecting it to his artificial knee on the other. The tension bearing spring hidden in the heel was meant for absorbing shock, but had been modified for other purposes. A steal mesh covered in white canvas surrounded the main braces in the shape of a normal calf and foot. If not for the fact that it was a second left leg, it would have aroused little suspicion from the casual observer. A final tap locked the bolt in place. Kuzen smiled and held out his hand for the guard to shake. The guard grasped a patch of empty air and shook it as though he were holding Kuzen's hand.

"I wish you luck at trial Kuzen. We all know what you said about the Queen three years ago and not all of us disapprove," he said with a sly grin.

"The Queen ain't who he used to be," Kuzen replied.

The guard nodded knowingly, then bound Kuzen and Thomas in plastic handcuffs and led them out of the holding area. Emerald green carpets led the defendants to their table situated to the right of the prosecution table and directly in front of the magistrate's podium. Two guards stood on either side of the defense table, while the prosecutor's table was bare. Witnesses, police officers, reporters, and men in dresses sat on seven rows of lacquered benches behind and to either side of the defendants table. Thomas and Kuzen sat on metallic folding chairs. Kuzen took considerable effort to sit due to his damaged prosthetic. The moment Kuzen sat, the guard to his left forced him to stand, then bow, while the Queen of England entered the room.

"The wondrous, glorious, not at all manly in the face Queen has decided to grace us with her presence as both the prosecution and judge," the bailiff announced.

"She's the prosecution and judge?" Thomas asked in an alarmed voice.

The Queen's grey eyes fixated on Kuzen. It spoke to Thomas, but did not look away from its prey.

"That is correct, defendant number one. We will read the list of charges. You will have a chance to defend yourself. Then We will dole out punishment as We see fit. And if you don't like that you can jolly well climb up Our ass and consume the pin worms from Our royal shit."

"Parasites from a parasite," Kuzen muttered.

The guard to his left coughed in order to cover Kuzen's insult. The Queen cleared its throat, spat into the bailiffs outstretched hand, and began to speak.

"Ladies, Gentlemen, men in dresses, and the Irish; these two hoodlums stand before you today on suspicion of the following charges. Defendants one and two; both for illegally entering British territory without written consent, evading arrest, assault on a baker's wife, and violating tea time. In addition, defendant number one is accused of brandishing an uncorked butter knife, antisemitism, and vandalizing a roaming camera, which as we all know exist for our own sense of decency and safety."

As the Queen spoke, four remote controlled cameras rolled beneath the benches. Three found women in short skirts. The fourth found a man in a dress and short-circuited. Three flying cameras darted over the royal head while cameras in each window and ceiling beam fixed upon the royal visage. It wore a bright red robe lined with zebra skin. The Queen stood about six foot seven inches with an added six inches of height due to the elaborate gold and diamond crown it wore. The royal adams apple stuck out nearly as long as the royal nose, which was broken and angled to the left. Hairy arms gave way to potato shaped hands that tapped melon colored fingernails against the varnished podium. Angry grey eyes fixed upon Kuzen from behind a shroud of dangling grey hair.

"And of course," the Queen continued. "Defendant number two is accused of insulting the monarchy three years earlier by suggesting that we aren't actually the Queen."

Kuzen smiled and said, "You forgot one thing."

"And what would that be?" the Queen replied.

"If you're going to walk around in ladies clothes, you should probably remember to tuck you cock and balls in like a big girl," Kuzen said while grinning and tapping his feet.

"I shall take that as an admission of guilt!" the Queen

screamed. "And how do you plead, defendant number one?" he asked while placing a bible in front of his bulge.

Thomas stood and straightened his brown suit. The room fell silent save for the sound of clicking heels approaching from a distant hallway.

"I see that your highness is a fair, and …beautiful woman. I know that if you look into your noble heart, you'll find the compassion to forgive us."

Two knocks sounded from the holding area door. The Queen stepped from the podium and put his hairy hands upon the defendant's table. Silverfish darted between the royal teeth. A yellow pustule on the royal lower lip burst and stained Kuzen's shirt.

"My compassion for the two of you begins with slow torture in private and ends with public execution," the He-Queen whispered.

Thomas and the guards trembled. Kuzen spat hot yellow phlegm onto the royal visage.

"Execution! I sentence these men to execution!" the Queen shouted at the top of his lungs while flipping the defendants table.

Thomas and Kuzen fell back. Witnesses made for the exits while police officers inflated their balloon batons. The Queen slapped a balloon out of the nearest officer's hands, retrieved a pistol from between the royal man boobs, and aimed for Thomas's heart.

"Oh no you don't mister miss thing!" a falsetto voice called from the holding room doorway.

There stood Joe, in an extravagant white satin, white fur lined dress with a high cut that exposed his extravagantly hairy left leg. He held a silver sequins covered pixie wand in one hand and his exposed testicles in the other. Kuzen lunged to his right and pushed Thomas behind the overturned defendant's table.

"I thought I had you killed Joseph," the Queen growled.

"Have at you, imposter!" Joseph screamed while he shook his pixie wand in the Queen's direction.

A horizontal beam of silver sequins struck the Queen in the eyes. Four balloon-wielding police officers launched in opposite directions as Joseph bounded through them. The Queen tried to clear his eyes but failed. Joseph shoved him to the floor and planted his beet red testicles against the royal forehead.

Balloon wielding police officers surrounded Thomas and Kuzen. Thomas stood and raised his fists. Kuzen pulled his hat over his brow and prepared to strike.

"Everyone cease this ridiculous behavior at once!" Joseph commanded as he continued to rub his massive, steaming testicles onto the Queen's forehead.

Brown foam poured from the Queen's mouth. Kuzen recognized Joseph and performed a textbook double take.

"Is that you, Lord GobKnobbler?" Kuzen asked. "Jesus, you're supposed to bite the pillow, not swallow it."

Witnesses returned to their seats. Officers deflated their batons and stood over the royal body.

"How do you know this man?" Thomas asked.

Kuzen reached out his hand for Lord GobKnobbler and

helped him to stand. When he was certain no one was looking, he wiped his hand on the back of an officer's jacket. The man in frilly women's clothing stepped forward and addressed Thomas directly.

"I am Lord Joseph GobKnobbler the Third, and rightful ruler of this country. That man with the terrible fashion sense on the floor is my half brother Jeb. Three years ago, he murdered my father and assumed his identity. Jeb thought he had paid our mutual friend Kuzen to murder me, but Kuzen helped me escape to America instead."

Joseph took Thomas by both hands and pressed them against his flabby man boobs. A hush fell over all other persons gathered in the room.

"Kuzen assisted me on the condition that I would help him find you. Unfortunately, we lost sight of each other during a crackdown on literacy and I ended up in a reprogramming camp. It wasn't until I saw Kuzen that day at the Hillary Clinton rally that I remembered my identity and the promise I made."

"But why me, why am I so important?" Thomas asked.

His hands shook. He found it difficult to keep his teeth from chattering.

"Is it really you, Lord GobKnobbler the Third?" A policewoman asked.

Joseph pointed towards the impostor's forehead where his testicles left a third degree burn. Joseph looked Thomas directly in the eyes and continued to speak. Tears gathered in Joseph's eyes. His syphilis scars trembled with emotion.

"Thomas, my lineage is that of English Queens. The members of my father's family are born with genitals that can reach temperatures exceeding four hundred degrees Fahrenheit. It is the blessing bestowed upon the GobKnobblers by our lineage. We alone can find partners of the ancient line. You see, as members of the ancient blood, our bodies are impervious to heat. You and I, Thomas, can withstand any trial by fire, so to speak. The blessing of your particular branch of the royal family is best left unspoken for the time being. Now is not the time to talk of such trivial things. Now is the time for celebration! Because you and Kuzen provided a distraction, and brought the imposter Queen from his fortified palace, I have won back my rightful place at the throne."

The police, the witnesses, and even Kuzen went to one knee and bowed their heads. Thomas meant to follow suit but Joseph grabbed Thomas's shoulder and forced him upright.

"And you Thomas, you are the rightful king of Ungland."

Joseph bowed his head and went to one knee. He reached into the back of his dress and pulled a red-hot silver ring from between his pimply butt cheeks. He placed it in Thomas's hand. Thomas recoiled, expecting it to sear his skin. But it produced no such effect. Joseph closed Thomas's hand around the ring and continued to speak.

"This silver band is the symbol of your heritage. Three years ago, the leaders of the world's free states were assassinated, imprisoned, or secretly replaced. You were among those leaders."

Thomas's mouth hung open. He found it difficult to breathe. Kuzen stood and bowed respectfully.

"His words are true my Lord," Kuzen began. "Your usurper announced that you had fallen overboard a hot air balloon while on a trip to America. This news followed your father's suspicious death in India by less than three weeks. I dredged the American coastline for months, in hopes of recovering your remains. Just as I was about to lose hope, I saw your face on a propaganda film extolling the supposed positive effects of the American reprogramming camps. They showed you rolling out of a plaster building and crawling onto a pile of hamburgers. You consumed at least twenty before passing out from diabetic shock." Kuzen paused and clenched his right hand upon his false leg before continuing. "It took years to find you Thomas. I had some great leads at first, but all proved dead ends. Between months of searching, I occasionally returned to Yurope to fight against the great change of power."

Kuzen bit his lip and took a deep breath before continuing. Several roaming cameras floated over his head. Joseph stepped in front of Kuzen and made his first royal decree.

"Shut down these nosy cameras! What a man does in the privacy of his house, heart, and rectum is none of the governments concern!"

He grabbed a flying helicopter and held it to his lips.

"Save for the really kinky stuff," he whispered. "Forward me a copy and burn the originals."

Floating cameras plummeted. Rolling cameras went limp beneath women's dresses.

"I had no idea things had gone so wrong while I was searching for you," Kuzen continued. "I see now how fortunate we have been to go through England instead of directly to Ungland. Now we have gathered an ally to help us in the fight against your usurper. Ungland is the last bastion of logic, freedom, and morality in the world. Your usurper means to transform it into a counterpart to modern Yurope and America. I have to know now Thomas. Seeing what you have, are you willing to continue to Ungland and depose the wicked king?"

Thomas grasped the burning red ring in his left hand and slipped it on his right hand ring finger.

"It's a perfect fit," he exclaimed.

"It was your father's. And since we're cousins, our love can… never be," Joseph replied.

Silent tears poured down Joseph's face, over a cluster of warts, and onto his exposed testicles where they boiled into stinking puffs of brown steam.

"There's just one thing I don't get," Kuzen said. "How did you follow us all this way? You didn't swim, did you Joe?"

Lord Joseph GobKnobbler the Third reached into his dress. All persons gathered took a step back in revulsion.

"Oh you silly goose's cunts!" Joseph said with a smile.

He reached further down into his dress and retrieved what resembled a stretched piece of moldy, sun-cooked leather. He held it to his face and Kuzen doubled over with laughter. With the leather in place, Joseph resembled the hag that molested Thomas aboard the Salted Clam. Cold vomit stirred in Thomas's stomach.

"It was me all along!" Joseph said while clicking his heels.

"That was one hell of a mask!" Kuzen exclaimed.

Joseph dropped the leathery object to the floor and replied, "Oh no, that was no mask. While The two of you waited for that boat to come ashore, I swam out to it, found this old hag taking a shit over the side of the boat, cut her to ribbons, fashioned a costume out of her rotting, stinking husk, and had a bit of fun when helping Thomas climb aboard."

His voice and expression were emotionless. Dried flecks of blood peeled from his cracked lips as he spoke.

"Well thanks," Thomas said as casually as he could manage

"It felt good Thomas," Joseph replied while nodding. "It was like Christmas in July in my foreskin."

"Well, anyways. We really need to get going now," Kuzen said while pulling Thomas towards the exit.

They took seven backwards steps together before Joseph called out for them.

"Wait, please! The Illegitimate King of Ungland must know that Thomas is alive by now. My bastard half brother Jeb would not have neglected to inform him."

As if on cue, the imposter Queen stood and made a break for the exit. He shoved a police officer aside and ran towards Thomas. Kuzen undid the bolt on his second left leg and thrashed Jeb to the floor.

"You can't possibly stop us now. There are a million times more of us than you," he spat.

Joseph stepped forward and tread upon the impostor's back.

"You will need more support than I can give you," he said with downcast eyes. "I shall provide you with a boat and an escort to France. There you must travel east and gather as many allies as you can on your way to Ungland. Just please, promise me you'll stay safe," Joseph continued.

His weary eyes fell upon Thomas's face, dropped to his crotch, then back to Thomas's face again.

"I'll keep him from harm," Kuzen said.

He leaned against Thomas and exited the building. A burst of cold English air struck them as they stepped outside.

"I thought we were as good as dead," Thomas said with a sigh.

"I had a back up plan," Kuzen grumbled while shaking his prosthetic leg in one hand.

Thomas took the false leg in hand and knelt in order to reattach it.

"I can do it myself," Kuzen said quickly.

The red-hot ring on Thomas's right hand brushed against Kuzen's skin and Kuzen jumped back three feet in pain.

"That blasted ring won't ever cool down!" he screamed. "I let your cousin carry it just for that reason. Do me a favor and keep that damned ring to yourself!" Kuzen said while reattaching his leg.

"Shouldn't you call me king or lord or something?" Thomas asked.

"Not until you've taken the crown," Kuzen replied, "Until then, you're just a deposed wanderer. And believe you me Thomas, you aren't the only one."

Thomas meant to ask for an explanation. However, heavy

footfalls on cobblestone interrupted their conversation. An ornate horse drawn carriage pulled up alongside them.

"Are you our escort?" Kuzen asked the minuscule man seated atop the carriage.

"Only to the sea," the driver replied.

Kuzen and Thomas climbed inside the carriage. There, they found and consumed several bowls of milky soup, ice cold tea, and unpalatable sandwiches. Their stressful morning, coupled with a lack of sleep, and overfull stomachs sent our heroes into deep and peaceful slumber. Some time later, their carriage came to an abrupt halt. Thomas fell out of his seat. Kuzen awoke with a cold cup of tea in his lap.

"Wasn't that a bit fast for crossing the entire British island?" Kuzen asked.

"I took a shortcut," the driver replied.

Kuzen and Thomas stepped outside.

"Feels good to stretch my legs," Thomas said.

"Good for you," Kuzen grumbled.

The carriage pulled away, leaving Thomas and Kuzen twenty feet from the ocean's edge and their transportation to France.

"Hello honey buns!" Joseph called out from the driver's seat of a pedal powered boat that resembled a massive swan.

The vessel bore the title "White Swallow" in lime green paint on the side.

"Isn't it a bit unrealistic to reach France by pedal boat?" Thomas inquired.

"I know a secret way in from behind," Joseph replied while winking and ripping a rancid fart.

Thomas lingered at the edge of the pier. Kuzen rolled his eyes and pushed Thomas aboard. Joseph immediately began to pedal. He tried to talk to Thomas several times, but the sound of his superhuman peddling drowned out any potential conversation. Low-lying clouds whizzed by on either sides of the vessel. A school of flying fish kept pace with the White Swallow and took turns jumping over our heroes. Twenty minutes later, they reached the coast of France. Blinding white light reflected off the freshly painted pier. Happy couples, painters, musicians, and an unusually tall mime came into view. Two young boys sat at the pier's edge, fishing for their lunch.

"Did you pedal all the way here from England?" The younger boy asked loudly as the White Swallow prepared to dock.

"I guess you could say I'm a real pedal-file!" Lord Joseph GobKnobbler the Third replied with a grin, a wink, and a fit of tuberculosis induced coughing.

"Hooray!" the elder of the boys cried.

"Yippee! We're going to get raped!" the youngest lad added as he and his friend climbed aboard the great swan boat.

Joseph raised his eyebrows and replied, "It isn't rape if you want it."

"Aw shucks," both boys said in unison.

Joseph put his arms around the boys and pulled them

close to his heaving body.

He took a deep breath and said, "It's ok. Once I start, you'll beg me to stop. But I won't. So THAT will be rape,"

"Yippee!" both boys replied.

They pranced about the deck, waiving white handkerchiefs over their heads.

"You can't be serious," Thomas said as he and Kuzen exited the boat.

"What can I say, I'm a man ruled by my appetites and I just love fresh little baguettes," Joseph replied.

He sat at the pedals and backed away from the coast.

"Don't be jealous Tommy-poo; we'll always have the Salted Clam!" Joseph added before the sound of his back peddling completely drowned out his voice.

He disappeared with the two French boys into a thick sea fog. Kuzen turned to Thomas and smiled. Thomas bent over and vomited into the sea.

8.

"So where do we start?" Thomas asked.

"Let's make nice with the locals," Kuzen replied.

A beautiful Parisian woman stood beside a lamppost.

"Excuse me, Mademoiselle?" Kuzen called.

She smiled at Kuzen, then grimaced and sprinted away. A smell like a thousand asses filled the air as a lanky mime in tattered clothing bounded towards Kuzen. The mime pinched its breast pocket and shook it as though something were vibrating from within. It then reached into that pocket and retrieved its hand with the thumb and pinky finger extended. Kuzen tried to step past the mime but it blocked his path and shook its hand by Kuzen's ear.

"Yeah I get it, your hand is a phone. My fist is about to be a toothbrush if you don't get out of my way!"

"I think he's saying the call is for you," Thomas said.

"Somehow I don't think we'll have much of a conversation."

"Come on Kuzen, play along. I bet he's going to do something funny!"

"Fine, let's just get this over with."

Kuzen held the gloved hand to his ear for ten seconds in silence.

"That's it? No punch line?"

Kuzen pulled away from the mime and saw the new shape of its outstretched hand. The over-sized middle finger seemed extra comical as it wiggled in the air. Kuzen balled his left hand into a fist and lunged forward. Thomas intervened and shoved both parties aside.

"This has to stop!" he cried. "The two of you are scaring the locals."

Parisians fled in every direction, froze in fear, or waved white handkerchiefs over their heads. "Je me rends!" some of them mumbled over and over again.

"What is that they're whimpering?" Kuzen asked.

Thomas tried to remember. He thought back through those two years of reprogramming and attempted to recall the schooling he received in his youth. Though he could remember neither classroom, classmates, nor teachers, the translation popped into his mind.

"They are surrendering."

The mime stood at least fifteen inches taller than Kuzen with a similar advantage of reach. As it shoved Thomas aside and lumbered over to Kuzen, its knuckles scraped the ground. Kuzen pressed a button on the side of his prosthetic leg that allowed him to lean upon it and store energy in a spring in the heel. The moment the mime came within reach, Kuzen pounced and struck repeated blows. French civilians fled the scene. A water laden cloud blocked out the sun.

"Please stop!" Thomas commanded.

Kuzen's hand hung in the air. Bright blood dripped from his torn knuckles and stained the mime's face. Sunlight burst through the dark cloud on the horizon. Kuzen looked into the mime's mouth and recoiled in fear. There, behind twin rows of yellow teeth, the gangrenous stump of a torn out tongue flailed in the mime's throat. The mime breathed heavily and shielded its face with its torn and bloodied gloves.

"What are you d-demanding of?" a faltering voice called from across the pier.

A policeman stood at the doorway of a cigarette shop with a bullhorn clutched in his trembling hands.

"What you w-want ever, just t-take it, person!" the policeman pleaded.

He slipped off his watch and tossed it to Kuzen. He then removed his skinny jeans and presented his anus as well.

"Just don't hurt us!" the policeman pleaded as a nervous, wet fart slipped betwixt his cheeks.

"I don't want any of that!" Kuzen announced while backpedaling.

He and Thomas locked eyes and nodded, then ran to a path opposite of the trembling policeman. The ocean lapped at a black pebble beach on their left. Local peasants grazed on snails and cheese wheels in a clearing to their right. An American tourist with a little American flag emblazoned backpack sat against a tall oak tree. She held a loaf of long French bread under each of her armpits and stained them with her gravy-scented sweat. Her immense bulk stressed the tree she leaned against to the point of breaking. Bits of brown bark cracked and fell upon her exposed, hotdog like shoulders. Two Parisian children ran around the tourist. A little boy grabbed a piece of bark from the sky and rubbed it against his left armpit.

"Is this how you use soap?" he asked.

"No stupid, you do it like this!" his sister replied while rubbing a strip of the bark against her teeth.

"Oh you poor, freedom hating savages. I am a modern, liberated woman. Therefore, I only wash my front butt, and only when I got a government appointed date," the tourist replied with a snort.

"My English is not so good. What is a government appointed date?" the French girl asked.

"That's when the government respects my right to have relations once a month with a white fellow whether he likes it or not. They break into his room, sedate him, and drive him right to my corn pile behind the MegaMart."

"Isn't that rape?" The boy asked in surprise.

"Ho ho ho!" The tourist laughed. "A woman can't rape a man. Besides, it's my body and my choice. Sure, they usually try to run away when the drugs wear off, but I'm already on top at that point. Nothing they can do but snack on some corn husks and enjoy the ride."

The tourist punctuated her answer with a long vinegary queef. The little girl gasped for air. Her brother tried to pull her away from the tourist but collapsed and choked on a throat full of bread and wine flavored vomit. The tourist inhaled her own pungent cervical perfume and smiled. She then reached into the bottom of her cut off jeans with both hands, scratched herself, retrieved a pubic louse, and ate it.

"Dear god, did you see that?" Thomas asked.

Kuzen looked over Thomas's shoulder and saw a blur of white and black approaching.

"We've got company!" he announced while pulling Thomas forward.

Thomas looked back and doubled in speed. The mime closed in on him like a hungry predator. Its blood-spattered face bore a strange smile that sent a shiver up Thomas's taint. Thomas took a sharp right and ran between a painter and his subjects. The main subject was a nude, elderly woman who held a bottle of chilled red wine between her shivering, hairy thighs. The secondary subject was a German man in full Nazi regalia. He filled a wine glass held between the woman's flabby breasts with his cold orange urine. Thomas accidentally knocked the sitting subject to the ground. The German laughed and urinated on her face.

"You really piss me off," Kuzen said as he grabbed the German by the arm and flung him backwards at the mime.

The mime slapped the German aside and jumped over the artist. The artist looked up and smiled as a cloud of bubbling backdoor booty butter rained upon him from the mime's soiled sweatpants. He pressed his brush to paint and began his painting with new inspiration and passion. A young French woman stood five feet ahead of Thomas. Though she was barely more than average in terms of looks, she had lips that could suck the foreskin back out of a circumcised dick. As Thomas approached, she grasped dark green slugs and snails in either hand.

"Are you touristing?" she asked in somewhat broken English.

"Not exactly," Thomas replied.

She smiled at Thomas and shoved a handful of mollusks into her mouth.

"Voulez-vous quelque chose de collant?" she asked while spitting bits of snail onto Thomas's suit.

"Sure thing Cheesecakes," Thomas replied while grabbing the remaining handful of snails.

The young French girl, from here on referred to as Cheesecakes, jabbed her long, slimy tongue towards Thomas's mouth. He turned to the side and cast the snails at the mime's feet and grimaced as Cheesecake's tongue penetrated his ear. The mime slid forward. Kuzen ducked and the mime flew over his back. Kuzen's hat fell to Thomas's feet. Thomas retrieved it with his foot and tossed it like a Frisbee. Kuzen caught it on his right index finger where it spun twice before coming to rest atop his balding head.

"Nice toss Kiddo," Kuzen began.

"Nice snatch," Thomas replied while checking out Cheesecake's dainty backside.

The mime stood between Thomas and Kuzen. Thomas led his French female friend aside and walked back to face the mime. Kuzen pulled his hat brim down to his nose and smiled.

"And who's the dame?" Kuzen asked.

Thomas smirked while wiping green slime from his ear.

"That's Cheesecakes. Her breath is awful but everything else is A-OK."

Cheesecakes stared in horror at the towering mime. Her first impulse was to run away. However, she saw Kuzen and Thomas stand their ground. If courage resides in a corner of the human heart, that corner grew ten fold that day in the young Parisian girl. Feeling empowered, Cheesecakes sprinted towards the American tourist.

"This one has enough yeasts, I think," she said.

She grabbed baguettes from the tourist's armpits and tossed them to Kuzen and Thomas.

"I was going to eat those. I need my nutrients or I'll starve!" the tourist screamed.

She curled into a ball and rolled to the side in order to face Thomas and Kuzen.

"I'm going to roll over you both and I won't roll off until you satisfy all my womanly needs and freedoms," she said while biting into a sore on her grey lower lip.

Fortunately, a slug scented fart escaped from Cheesecakes' pearly pink shit cave and struck the tourist in the face. She rolled backwards three full rotations in surprise and plunged twenty feet down a steep and rocky hill. She bounced twice before continuing to roll and came to a stop atop a crushed picnic basket. Cheese wheels and slug flesh spread onto the ground around the tourist. She smiled and began to eat. The young French boy, whose picnic she had ruined, began to scold her in French. His parents stopped him, removed their jewelry, and presented their posteriors towards the tourist. She giggled and continued to feast. A tall shadow fell over the tourist from the top of the hill. The mime stepped towards Kuzen and Thomas in floppy black and white shoes.

"We're not running any further," Kuzen said as the mime closed in.

"That's far enough!" Thomas cried while brandishing his long French bread.

The mime took another step forward. Thomas and Kuzen thrust their baguettes at the mime. He slapped Kuzen's loaf aside. It flew through the air and lodged into the surrendering French man's anus. He kept his head low and stayed immobile, even as the tourist nibbled his anally impaled baguette.

"We aren't going to surrender, if that's what you wanted," Kuzen said while pulling the brim of his hat over his brow.

Thomas thought back to his schooling and translated as best as he could.

"Nous n'abandonnerons pas," he said while looking the Mime in the eye.

The mime stepped forward and smiled. He removed his over-sized gloves and held out his exposed left hand. Cracked cream-colored paint covered the mime's calloused fingers. Thomas took a step forward and held out his hand.

"You can't be serious," Kuzen objected.

Thomas grasped the mime's hand and shook it. His red-hot ring singed the mime's hand paint. The mime appeared otherwise unaffected.

"I think he's been looking for someone that wouldn't back down," Thomas said.

The mime smiled and nodded.

"So you understand English after all?" Kuzen asked.

The mime held its thumb and forefinger an inch apart.

"He only knows somewhat little," Cheesecakes

interpreted.

Thomas and Cheesecakes laughed. The mime held his sides and imitated the motions of laughter in silence.

"Well this is great? Now we're just one big stinky French family huh," Kuzen said.

"Well, you said you wanted to make nice with the locals," Thomas replied.

"This isn't what I meant. An over-sized clown and an oversexed teenager aren't going to help us against your usurper," Kuzen added.

Cheesecakes furrowed her brow. The mime held out his hand to Kuzen and pointed at its palm. Sunlight faltered. No one could see the mime's explanation.

9.

Tremendous grey blimps cruised overhead. Wires dangled beneath them. Sparks burst between the wires as a five hundred foot wide and three hundred foot tall image took shape. Hillary Clinton sat at a varnished desk with a cheeseburger in either hand.

"Looks like Hillary won the election," Thomas said.

"Well of course she won. Any one that tried to run against her was accused of misogyny and castrated!" Kuzen replied.

"My fellow Americans and future Americans subjects," Hillary began.

Cheesecakes read the French translation at the bottom of the floating screen. The mime put his hands over his heart and trembled. A flock of geese flew through the projection of Hillary's mouth and burst into flames. As she continued to speak, it looked as though she were eating them alive.

"Too long have we tolerated those that are not like us. It has come to my attention that a certain man has threatened the ideals and freedoms we cherish the most. Freedoms, such as liberty, forced castration, welfare, and of course, baby burgers, the burgers made by infants, for infants, of infants."

"Sweet merciful bouncing baby Jesus, let's get them!" the cameraman interrupted.

Hillary held out her left hand and shook her head. With her right hand, she put a baby burger to her lips and pretended to take a bite.

"Even you could fake it better than that," Kuzen said

while poking the Mime with his right elbow.

As soon as Kuzen looked away, the Mime silently mimed eating a burger. Hillary set down her burgers and pulled a red white and blue pistol from her desk drawer.

"I know that I have previously expressed distaste for war. Literacy, free thought, and self-sufficiency hold back humanity and give unfair advantages to those willing to work in order to attain them. These wars of thought damage our proud nation and its citizens alike. However, these rogue nations and their leader leave us with little alternative."

Hillary loaded her pistol as she spoke. An image of Thomas appeared over her shoulder.

"This criminal has already deposed the rightful Queen of England. We believe he intends to spread his hateful message of self-respect and self-sufficiency as far as the golden land of Ungland. We shall leave no stone unturned, no book unburned, no pork product uneaten until his capture; even if that requires invading our allies in Ungland. Like our forefathers, foremothers, and forepersons of indiscriminate gender, we will take arms and take action! If not for similar actions in the past, we would all be speaking British today."

Hillary flashed a reptilian smile in anticipation of an outburst of applause from the American public. That smile twitched into a frown before she continued speaking.

"With my first act as President of these United States I hereby declare war on all freedom hating nations. This operation shall be, from this date forward, referred to as Operation: My Body, My Army, My Choice. All relatively able-bodied American citizens are to report to their local reprogramming stations for warfare programming and wheelchair retrofitting. To all non Americans watching this message, surrender immediately if you wish to live."

Hillary pointed her pistol backwards and shot the image of Thomas between the eyes.

"Otherwise, may OUR God have mercy on YOUR likely non-existing, brown person souls."

Flames ran up the wires as they disconnected from the blimps and fell onto the gathering crowd. Cheesecakes and the mime trembled. All other French persons fled. Cheesecakes clutched Thomas's brown lapels and peered into his weary hazel eyes.

"She'll have every of us killed to pursuit of you. Why?" she asked.

"The enslaved will always begrudge a man that is free," Kuzen replied under his breath.

Their conversation faded into an eerie silence that only the American tourist could break.

"Serves you losers right for hating our freedoms!" she cried.

She punctuated her statement with a long, wavering belch that transitioned into projectile vomiting. Once the vomiting ceased, she gathered her bile with both hands and shoveled it back into her gaping maw. Thomas placed his hands upon Cheesecakes' shoulders. His red-hot ring singed her dress.

"Is there no salvation to hope?" she asked.

Thomas wanted to comfort her, but the mime had other plans. It knelt in mud and pressed it's face against Thomas's ring.

"You let him go right now you sniveling zebra's cunt!" Kuzen barked.

"Yes, you leave handsome brave man alone!" Cheesecakes chimed in.

The mime glanced at Thomas's, who nodded knowingly.

"Have you forgotten about my ring Kuzen?" Thomas asked.

"You can't possibly mean," Kuzen began.

"Don't you see how the searing silver has no effect on his skin? This mime must be a GobKnobbler."

The mime stood and shook its head disgustedly.

"No Thomas. Each branch of the true royal family has a title of their own. Only the British are considered GobKnobblers," Kuzen replied.

"So what am I to call my new found friend?" Thomas asked.

The mime placed its hands on Thomas's shoulders. As Kuzen spoke, it mouthed its name in unison.

"Pitre Tumbickler," Kuzen replied. "Though the Tumbicklers held no official power in France, they were highly esteemed by the public. Around the time of your father's death, late party guests found the Tumbicklers murdered in their castle. What should have been a celebration for the eldest son, Pitre Tumbickler's engagement, became a crime scene instead. Something caused the Tumbickler's tongues to swell until they suffocated. Pitre was the only Tumbickler unaccounted for following the murders. Only his tongue on a dinner plate remained."

Grey droplets formed in the corners of the mime's eyes.

"Is this true, Pitre?" Thomas asked.

The mime nodded. Kuzen and Cheesecakes looked into the mime's eyes. Pitre caught their gaze and looked away. His eyes seemed to falter and have no particular focus.

"And, was your bride murdered as well?" Thomas asked while pressing Pitre's hand.

Pitre shook his head, then placed his right arm around Cheesecake's shoulder and made a motion as if he was drinking a glass of wine. He took Cheesecake's right arm by the elbow, and motioned as though she were putting something into his glass as he looked away. He took another imaginary sip and fell to his knees. Pitre grasped Cheesecake's left foot and drove it into his own rib-cage. He then frowned and mimed biting off his own tongue.

"So she betrayed you," Kuzen whispered.

Pitre nodded.

"But why?" Thomas asked.

Pitre's entire face puckered into a frown. He raised one soiled glove and pointed down the road. There, beyond several rows of houses and shops, stood a tall white building atop a ten-foot tall grassy hill. Hundreds of civilians gathered at the base of the hill, though none dared to climb to the top.

"Who lives there?" Thomas asked.

Kuzen reached into his jacket pocket for a cigarette. He found only an empty carton and grimaced.

"Following the assassination of the Tumbickler family, the positions of president and prime minister were combined under the order of president elect Sper Medrinke. The new position, called the Prime President, included all powers and authorities of president, prime minister, parliament, and head of the military."

"Why didn't anyone try to stop him?" Thomas asked.

Cheesecakes looked down at her feet. Kuzen took a deep breath before he continued.

"Medrinke fought resistance to his proposal via fear. He ran an add campaign, reminding the public of what had become of the Tumbickler family. At the time of the murders, it was widely believed that one of the Tumbicklers was going to run against Sper. His official reason for grabbing power was to remove any motivation for an underling to arrange his assassination."

Having relived the worst moment of his life, Pitre had little desire to rise on his own; but Cheesecakes pulled Pitre onto his knees so that they were face to face.

"The woman that betrayed you, you can't mean first lady, Cu Medrinke, can you?" she asked in French.

Pitre reached into his jacket pocket and retrieved two golden rings. One was pristine and new, as though worn for a very short time and cast aside. The other was grayed and cracked, as though worn for a great deal of time and removed only by force.

"That's the way it is with women," Kuzen rasped.

He turned and walked towards the Prime President's estate.

"What do you mean by that?" Thomas cried over the growing blare of sirens.

Kuzen stood beneath a streetlight and waited for Thomas, Pitre, and Cheesecakes to catch up to him. Thomas and Cheesecakes pulled Pitre along by his hands. His over-sized shoes left grey smears upon the pavement. Kuzen reached down and felt the bolt on his false leg.

"Women are always the first to demand a commitment. And are also the first to break that commitment the moment a better offer comes along," he said before withdrawing his hand.

"You sound bitter and defeated," Cheesecakes said.

"The Unglish never admit defeat; never give an inch, and never wallow in past failures," Kuzen replied.

Whether he intended his words for Cheesecakes, Thomas, or Pitre, none could tell. Pitre sniffled loudly as he stood, then glared at the tall white building in the distance. A stout man and a petite woman watched him from a window on the fourth floor. Pitre pointed towards them and spat grey phlegm into the wind. His bolus of lung butter flew over the side of several buildings. Where it would land, none could tell.

"Are you ready now?" Thomas asked.

Pitre raised one hand as if holding a hammer and brought it down into his palm. Kuzen readied the spring in his false heel. Pitre took Thomas and Cheesecakes by either hand. Twenty-six police officers stood on the road ahead. They formed a human chain and watched Thomas's company with glassy eyes. One of them raised a bullhorn and was about to speak. However, Pitre's phlegm descended from the sky and struck that policeman directly in the penis. The policeman collapsed. His twenty-five partners dropped to the ground and presented their disgusting, unwashed asses.

"Now!" Kuzen shouted.

They sprinted forward together through the throngs of despairing civilians. Pitre slung Thomas and Cheesecakes forward like twin whips and they slapped several officers on the ass while passing them by. They pushed their way to the base of the hill until they felt their lungs would burst. A grey haze hung in the air from distant fires. Thomas felt it sizzle against his ring.

"Has the invasion already beginning?" Cheesecakes asked.

"No, they'll have to go through England first," Kuzen replied.

"Are you sure?" she asked.

Kuzen did not respond. He took a handful of hill in hand and climbed towards the top. Pitre followed suit and overtook Kuzen easily. He reached down his spindly arms for Thomas to grasp. Thomas took Pitre's hand and was instantly flung to the top of the hill.

Thomas cried, "Oh crap!" and flailed his limbs before striking the ground.

Pitre reached back down for Cheesecakes and attempted to smile. She looked so sullen and defeated; he could not help but try to cheer her up. Pitre slid down the hill on his belly and came to a rest at Cheesecake's feet.

"Your act won't work on me," Cheesecakes croaked in French. "Going inside won't change anything. Even if we rough up the Prime President, the people will just pick another weak leader. It wont be long long before we're crushed beneath America's flabby thumb."

Pitre lifted one leg over an imaginary obstacle and rested his other leg in mid air. He then held out his hand for Cheesecakes to grasp.

"I'm not getting on your bike, there isn't enough magic in the world to get me up that hill," she replied in french.

Thomas kneeled and prepared to clamber down the ledge. Kuzen grasped Thomas by the shoulder and pulled him back onto his feet.

"That isn't necessary," Kuzen said. "The Tumbicklers have a special talent that few have seen in person."

"Like Joseph's red hot balls?"

"Technically, yes," Kuzen replied while pinching the bridge of his nose and shaking his head.

Pitre took Cheesecakes by the arm. In one swift pull, he lifted her over his shoulders and set her down on a pocket of air behind his back.

"They're floating!" Thomas said.

He grabbed Kuzen's jacket and shook it twice.

"Pipe down and watch," Kuzen whispered.

Cheesecakes looked down with wide, unbelieving eyes. Pitre pumped his legs against invisible pedals and rode up the side of the hill with Cheesecakes in tow. He grasped Kuzen and Thomas under his arms as he reached the top and continued peddling forward. A black policeman stood before the Prime Presidential estate entrance with a bullhorn clutched in one hand and a basketball in the other.

"Cut that shit out please. This is the only job I could get and they already yelled at me for coming in late this morning!" he said in a whimpering voice.

Pitre pedaled forward before slamming on his imaginary breaks. The policeman tossed the ball at Pitre. Pitre mimed shooting an arrow at the ball and it popped in mid air. They slid several feet across the white marble pathway, and stopped four inches from the policeman.

The policeman screamed, "Fuck this shit!" and ran away.

Pitre set down Thomas and Kuzen at the entrance. He noticed the black policeman eyeing his imaginary bike from behind a bush and locked it up with an imaginary chain. Cheesecakes alone stayed seated.

"Aren't you coming in with us?" Thomas meant to ask but Kuzen covered Thomas's mouth with his hat.

Pitre looked at Cheesecakes and smiled. He held out his over-sized glove. She hesitated, then grasped it. Pitre and Cheesecakes walked inside together. Somehow, it seemed natural, as though they were walking into their own marital home.

"Looks like I've been dumped," Thomas said while shaking his head.

"It could have been worse," Kuzen replied as he headed for the door.

"How so?"

"At least you still have both legs."

Thomas scratched the back of his head and followed Kuzen inside. The interior of the Prime Presidential Estate was pristine white with silver glistening from every corner. A silver vase with silver dipped roses sat atop a white marble piano. White couches with silver legs stood between silver framed paintings. Kuzen and Thomas's filthy boots left Parisian soil on the white marble floor.

"Where do you think we'll find the Prime President?" Thomas asked.

Kuzen struck the brim of his hat with his finger. Thomas looked upwards. The ceiling of the entrance ascended five floors. Openings with silver railings cast pale light into the rooms beyond, save for the fifth floor, which was pitch-black and without furnishings. Thomas looked to his left and saw Pitre climbing an imaginary rope. Cheesecakes followed him closely via a transparent elevator.

"How does he do that?" Thomas asked.

"You'd rather not know."

"Can I do that?"

"No. And if you could, I'd rather you didn't," Kuzen replied as he climbed five white marble steps and stood before the base of the transparent elevator.

Thomas scratched his head again and watched Pitre clamber over the fourth floor railing. The elevator descended quickly. Cheesecakes was not inside. Thomas stepped inside, stood next to Kuzen, and pressed the fourth floor button. They ascended slowly, passing a series of large impressionistic paintings on the opposite wall as they did so. The first floor painting depicted a short man felling a giant by cracking a bottle over its head. The short man's eyes were shrunken and lonely. A crimson shadow spread out beneath his feet.

"Why do you think Pitre didn't join Cheesecakes in the elevator?" Thomas asked.

Kuzen stifled a laugh and replied, "He probably didn't think she could stand the smell."

Thomas replied "huh" and scratched his head a third time.

As he did so, the second and third floor paintings passed by in a blur. The elevator stopped at the fourth floor. Kuzen straightened his suit and stepped into a hallway. Thomas peered through the transparent wall at the fourth floor painting. It depicted the short man standing upon a map of France. His expression was defeated and indifferent. A dark red, intricately detailed, shadow grew from beneath his feet. In comparison to the short man, that shadow seemed to have fifty times as many brush strokes. Thomas peered upwards to see the fifth floor painting. He saw an orange blur beyond the blackness. Before Thomas could make out the image, Kuzen grabbed him by the back of the collar and pulled him from the elevator. Thomas turned around and casually fixed his collar. Kuzen led Thomas to a tall crimson door and cleared his throat.

"Just let me do the talking," Kuzen said suddenly. "We came here to make allies, not friends. If things turn for the worse for Pitre, we may have to court the favor of Sper Medrinke and his bride. Don't you agree?"

Thomas pushed open the door and turned around to face

Kuzen.

"I'll take a clown over a murderer," he replied.

"Good answer," Kuzen whispered.

He walked past Thomas and into the room. Thomas and Kuzen stood on the skinny side of a partition wall. The left edge of a large pane of glass lit the way forward. As Thomas and Kuzen stepped into the main area of the room, they found Sper Medrinke on his knees. Cheesecakes and Pitre stood before him. The first lady stood off to the right and stared out of the window.

"Why did you do it?" Cheesecakes asked in French.

"I had no choice!" Sper replied.

"You getting any of this?" Kuzen asked.

"I'll fill you in on the juicy bits later," Thomas replied quietly.

He squinted and tried his best to keep up with the conversation. Fortunately, the first lady was silent and Pitre was mute.

"What do you mean that you had no choice?" Cheesecakes asked.

"I mean, had I not done as I was told, I would have shared in the fate of the Tumbicklers!" Sper replied.

"I don't believe that vile propaganda!" Cheesecakes screamed.

Pitre stared at the silent first lady's back. Sper took a deep breath and sighed.

"If I didn't agree to cover up the murders and take Madam Cu as my bride, she would have murdered me as she had her husband to be."

Thomas gasped. Kuzen pricked up his ears but understood nothing. Pitre took a step forward and placed his left hand on the first lady's left shoulder from behind.

"But he lived," Cheesecakes said through chattering teeth.

Pitre grasped the shoulder pad of Cu's crimson dress and mouthed Cheesecake's next question in unison.

"Why?"

Cu turned around to face Pitre. She was as beautiful as the day she poisoned his wine. No, she was even more beautiful. A lone grey tear rolled down Pitre's white plaster face. Cu reached up and caught the tear with a crimson fingernail. She flung it to the floor and opened her crimson lips to speak.

"I thought that I could control you Pitre. Convincing you to run for president assured me of that. But when I asked if you would assume other powers, you failed to surrender to my will."

"But why murder the Tumbicklers?" Cheesecakes asked.

Cu took a step backwards and pressed her back against the tremendous window.

"Because I could no longer stand the foul source of his putrid sorcery. I'm glad I killed the Tumbicklers. Their kind should never be allowed to poison the atmosphere!"

Thomas stepped forward but Pitre gestured for him to

wait.

Pitre held out his hands and signed, "I loved you."

Cu responded with an upheld middle finger. Pitre turned his back on Cu in order to walk away. Five hundred and forty three Frenchmen and women watched from the grassy hill as Cu Medrinke pulled a silver pin from the back of her dress and jumped bare-assed onto Pitre's shoulders. She jabbed the pin into his neck, where it struck the side of Pitre's massive Adams apple and bent. Pitre backed his faithless bride to be against the large glass window and bent at the knees. Five hundred and forty three Frenchmen and women stared in awe at the first lady's glorious double pressed ham. Cu kicked and tore and swore at Pitre. He calmly extended his arms as though he was falling from a great height. Imaginary wind tussled locks of his filthy grey hair. He grasped an imaginary ring from his shirt and pulled. Nothing happened. He looked at the imaginary ring in his hand in a pantomimed panic. Pitre pulled out his empty pockets, as though looking for another ring to pull. He then held up his right index finger and winked to Thomas.

"Don't you dare!" Cu screamed.

Pitre reached into his pants, grasped his backwards facing, shit brown penis, and pulled. A full on flatus fusillade followed. The steaming blanket of gaseous shit shot Cu backwards through the large glass window. She could have grasped onto Pitre, but covered her nose with both hands instead. Pitre went a few feet into the air and floated down slowly, as though supported via an invisible parachute. Cu fell to her death among the gathered crowd. A medium sized grey blimp floated up to the Prime Presidential estate and swallowed Cu in its shadow. Two medium length cables descended and fizzled until an image appeared between them. Hillary Clinton peered into the Prime presidential estate from her micro thin screen.

"We have breached the British coast," Hillary began.

Her booming voice hurt Thomas's ears. Pitre and Cheesecakes walked to the window in order to read the subtitles. Kuzen stayed on the other side of the room and pulled his wide brimmed cap over his face. As Hillary continued to speak, he reached down and grasped his artificial leg.

"It won't be long before they are defeated. You know what it is I want."

Sper Medrinke crawled to the broken window and peered down at his murdered bride.

"If you surrender now, I will guarantee your safety and a place in my new world order Sper," Hillary continued.

Sper stood and straightened his back. For the first time since the Great Change of Power, he looked and felt like an upright man. Sper placed one hand to his mouth and cleared his throat, then replied in the best English he could manage.

"I surrender," he began.

Hillary flashed a hungry smile that seemed to stretch beyond the corners of her mouth.

"That is," Sper continued. "I surrender to the one true king of France, Pitre Tumbickler!"

Cries of disbelief erupted from the crowd. Hillary rolled her eyes and cursed at an assistant off camera as her image blipped from the screen. The blimp released its black coils and hung still in the air. Hillary's voice rang out from the blimp one last time.

"Vais tous vous tuer," she said.

Or as Thomas translated aloud, "I will kill you all,"

Pitre smiled at the crowd.

"That man is no Tumbickler!" a woman shouted while her husband braided her armpit hair.

"He's nothing but a half rate mime!" a man wearing lime green skinny jeans replied.

Pitre took Cheesecakes by the arm and gestured for her to walk with him into the empty space beyond the broken window. She took a deep breath and held it. Not from fear, but from knowing the smell that was to come. She and Pitre stepped forward onto invisible steps created by the downwards force of Pitre's silent flatulence. A hush fell upon the crowd; particles of feces also fell upon the crowd, but mostly a hush.

"They look good together," Kuzen said as he joined Thomas at the window.

They then turned back and headed for the elevator. Before they descended, Thomas looked up at the fifth floor painting. Orange paint filled out the boarders, a smear of silver covered the bottom third. The remainder of the canvas was left unpainted.

Every French man and woman present kneeled before Pitre as Thomas and Kuzen exited the estate. Cheesecakes made to kneel as well, but Pitre stopped her and went to one knee instead. He reached into his pants and retrieved two golden rings. He held out the pristine ring for Cheesecakes to take. She glanced at Thomas and smiled sheepishly, then turned back toward Pitre and slipped the ring onto her porcelain finger. Pitre put the cracked ring onto his own ring finger and held his hand beneath his ass. He blasted the ring with a cloud of red-hot anal ambergris. When he retrieved his hand and held it in the air, his reforged ring shone beautifully in the sun.

"So a King takes a Queen and leaves a wanderer on his lonesome," Kuzen said while staring at the motionless blimp.

"I still have one friend," Thomas replied.

He took a deep breath, walked past Kuzen, stood before Pitre and bowed slightly before speaking.

"I am Thomas, the rightful heir to the throne of Ungland. I mean to reclaim my throne and fight with everything I have against Hillary's invasion. Will you and your people stand beside me?" Thomas asked.

Pitre held out his disgusting shit covered hand for Thomas to shake. Thomas grit his teeth and shook it.

"But how will we fight the Americans?" a peasant asked.

Pitre rolled up his sleeve and mimicked flexing a massive muscle. He then gestured for the peasants to clear a path between his backside and the blimp. Pitre bent over and aimed his bloody anus towards the blimp. Cheesecakes ran over and fed an imaginary cannonball into Pitre's bottom. She then lit an imaginary fuse atop his head and pulled her dress up to her face in order to shield her nose. A concentrated blast escaped from Pitre's rectum. The blimp exploded and shot tiny grey fragments of cloth across the sky. The gathered Parisians stood straight for the first time in years. Men and women held each other, not in fear, but in a shared feeling of strength and pride. The American tourist rolled towards the back of the group.

"That was disgusting!" she said while rolling into a French man's legs.

She saw a discarded French fry on the bottom of his boot and attempted to lick it free. The French man turned to face the tourist. His first instinct was to allow the American to eat his boot. However, he thought of his king's return and kicked the tourist in the face instead. His foot lodged into the tourist's skin like a mammoth stuck in tar. Five other French men ran over and kicked the tourist as well. Their combined efforts sent her rolling away. She rolled over Cu Medrinke's remains and crashed with her into a fountain on the other side of town. Thomas stood before Cheesecakes, but made certain to stay a respectable distance apart.

"Before we head off for Germany, could you at least tell me your real name?" he asked.

Cheesecakes opened her mouth to speak. However, Pitre swiveled his rectum towards Thomas and prepared to fire a second volley.

Kuzen ran forward and screamed, "He's not hitting on her!"

He arrived at Thomas's side just in time. Pitre's putrid posterior plume propelled our protagonists to perilous heights. Beautiful white buildings, the kind Thomas would have liked to build, passed beneath them. After flying horizontally, for what seemed like hours, they began to descend. Thomas and Kuzen screamed. Their screams however, proved unnecessary. Before they realized it, they had already floated softly to the ground. A parachute of flatulence fell upon them. Twisting their noses, they sprinted towards breathable air.

10.

Beyond a veil of wrought-iron fences, little white buildings peppered the horizon. A placard affixed to the nearest gate read "Holocaust Museum #347". Below that, a second placard read "Goyim Entry $20. Bubalas get in free!" Thomas and Kuzen headed for the gate. They passed rusted railroad tracks, deteriorating pole barns, and a half filled pool along the way.

"Can you believe the barbarism of them Germs?" someone asked.

A tall, bow legged man, stood behind our heroes. Cold winds tussled the wiry grey beard that swayed between his knobby knees, revealing his mangled, blood stained penis. He wore no clothing save for a diamond-encrusted yarmulke. His long, veiny nipples hung from his flabby chest like antennae and vibrated with the beating of his canary sized heart. A feint brown stain, born from his habit of wiping left to right, wrapped around his backside like a ring of rust. Thomas's eyes went wide. Kuzen studied the newcomer's reflection in the still waters of the pool.

"Follow my lead," he whispered.

Thomas nodded. Kuzen turned back.

"Seems you were expecting us Lord Gila," Kuzen said.

"Of course, no matter how busy I get, I always make time for showing goyim the errors of their ways. Now please, show me your entry passes and we can begin the tour of this horrific abomination against decency and morality that all good gentiles should witness in exchange for a nominal fee."

"You were saying something about the pools?" Thomas

interjected.

Kuzen smirked. Gila stood beside him. His haggard features reflected in the placid waters. He clenched his fists so hard that a half-digested matzo ball rolled out of his anus, down his bowed leg, and into the pool. Ripples contorted Gila's reflection as he began to speak.

"As a fourth generation holocaust survivor, I am kept awake most nights by the memories of films about those horrible times. Those god damned Germs lined us up in front of this pool of death, and drowned us one at a time."

"This water looks a bit shallow for that, don't you think?" Kuzen asked.

Gila turned towards Kuzen, red in the face, but took a deep breath and continued.

"People were shorter in those days. I'll have you know that my Great-Great Grandmother was drowned in that pool at least twice a week. We still pass around her old arm floaties once a year on the anniversary of her death. Luckily she managed to sneak them out in her luggage after the war."

"But you just said," Thomas interrupted.

Kuzen elbowed him in the ribs.

"Come with me, I'll show you two the showers next," Gila continued.

Thomas peered at Kuzen, who gestured for Thomas to follow. The three men passed a mural that depicted Adolf Hitler punching a puppy in the ribs. The next mural they passed depicted American actor Mel Gibson with an open mouth of dagger-like teeth. Hebrew, German, and English script below his chin read "Free Speech, Hate Speech, War." A third mural covered the exterior of the building Gila meant to enter. It depicted a Jewish man and woman squeezing a rainbow out of a black infant with a caption that read, "Tolerance and Unity Via Instigation and Manipulation." Gila stood before a screen door and peered back at Thomas.

"Prepare yourself for a well deserved pang of goy guilt," he said before stepping inside.

"Who is that?" Thomas asked when he and Kuzen were alone.

"Maybe an ally, probably not," Kuzen replied before stepping inside.

Thomas entered last. The smell of lavender struck him first. An overwhelming wave of body odor followed. Gila grabbed Thomas by the wrist and compelled him towards a row of shower-heads that lined a tiled wall.

"See these barbaric tools!" Gila shouted.

"Shower heads?" Thomas replied.

"Do either of you know how detrimental soapy water is to a desert dwellers skin? My great-grandfather took a schvitz once a year and they expected him to take a shower each day!"

"He should have eaten more fiber," Kuzen quipped.

"I said schvitz, you know nothing goy! A steam bath, the kiss of Yahweh! And it wasn't just water that poured from these metallic death devices. Those monsters would gas our chosen peoples, killing them! German guards used to stand outside and watch the steam rise through the open windows and screen doors. Depending on the type of Jews being murdered, the gas would be a different color. My Great-Great Grandfather wrote in his diary, which can be purchased at one of our gifts shops for a very reasonable fee, that when he was gassed to death, the steam was blue!"

Gila pounded his fists against the wall and pressed his forehead against the tile. He turned towards Thomas while gasping for breath.

"I remember being just a little God's-Chosen-Person, and watching the films of the great Steven Spielberg and his contemporaries. Not only did they provide me a stunning interpretation of my people's history, but were thoughtful enough to dictate exactly how I, the viewing audience, should feel about each film. Those that criticized or failed to praise the films enough were black listed, ridiculed, and occasionally forcibly circumcised. Those great directors of the past surely moved as the hands of Yahweh. Through the use of propaganda, guilt, lawsuits, and charging reasonable fees, they managed to turn entire societies towards their cause. Still, free thinkers poison the well of humanity. They use critical thought and free speech against my people's, wounding them deeply. Don't you just feel terrible thinking about it?" he asked.

Thomas peered over Gila's shoulders at Kuzen, who nodded.

"Sure," Thomas replied.

"Neat," Kuzen added.

"Thus concludes our tour. I fear I have only enough strength to take the two of you to the gift shop before retiring to my quarters. Perhaps you will both be so kind as to remember my sufferings when calculating your tips."

"So you really don't know who we are?" Kuzen asked.

"Of course I do," Gila replied. "You are the two goyim from Sweden that reserved my reasonably priced guided tour of this facility. No one else would have been permitted within these walls at this hour. Why, the last dumb schnook I caught trying to sneak in for free is still hanging from the flag pole by the gift shop."

Kuzen looked sidelong at Thomas and stepped between him and their guide as they exited the showers. They walked a cracked concrete path towards a single story building and a tall, wrought iron fence. Though Thomas glanced at the fence, Kuzen pulled him towards the gift shop entrance by the elbow.

"Let's see this one through," Kuzen whispered as they all stepped inside.

Hardback copies of Anne Frank's Diary, Anne Frank's Diary 2: Electric Jewgaloo, and Cooking with Foreskin, lined the walls to either side of the door. Various baseball caps, mugs, and t-shirts with slogans like "Good Goy", "I Visited Holocaust Museum #347 and All I Got Was This Luxuriously Crafted, Reasonably Priced T-Shirt", and "Oh No Jew Didn't!" lined the furthest wall.

The tour guide brushed past our heroes and stood before a silver plated cash register.

"Just show me your passes before I ring you goys up. I'll stamp them with this here stamper device, and every third stamp will earn you two percent off your next foreskin removal!"

Thomas meant to speak, but Gila cut him off.

"I know what you're going to say. You think you've already been snipped. But that's just a matter of Semitic semantics. Any skin between the head and balls is unnecessary for goyim. Besides, you were likely snipped with some awful metal tools. You'll never please Yahweh fully until you are trimmed down there by the teeth of an expert, reasonably priced, Jewish craftsman."

Havana smiled as he spoke, revealing a mouth filled with yellow, crooked teeth. Bloodied pubic hairs trembled between his teeth with every breath he took. Thomas took a step back. Kuzen unknowingly crossed his legs. Just then, the gift-shop door swung open. Two blonde haired, blue-eyed men walked into the building. One of them approached a deerskin lamp labeled "My Great-Great Grandmother's Skin" and began to weep.

The second man stood beside him and said, "I have never felt so tolerant, progressive, and guilty in my entire life."

"No way, I feel way more tolerant and guilty than you!" the weeping man replied.

"I gave my seat on the bus to a black woman."

"You assume xhe identifies as a woman, thus, discriminating against xer!"

The standing man fell to his knees, toppling a stack of golden teeth and foreskins in the process. He wept beside his friend so hard that his panties began to tear.

"We are the guiltiest men from Sweden, save for our fathers whom we resent!" they cried in unison.

"Wait just a second," Gila began to say while reaching into his beard.

Kuzen pulled Thomas towards the door.

"Get those Goyim!" Gila's voice screamed via a loudspeaker.

Thomas glanced over the gift shop roof, towards the source of the sound. Ravens circled the speakers at the top of a weather worn flag pole. Below that, a rotting human carcass swung by the neck from a scabby chain. Dozens of men poured from buildings on the far side of the complex. Thomas and Kuzen slipped through a sliding gate just before it slammed shut, entered a forest, and ran for what felt like hours. Many times, they heard or imagined they heard pursuing footsteps, despite exhaustion, they continued forward. Thomas tripped on a white stone and stumbled into daylight. German soil spread out to the horizon. White stones of crumbled castles cut through the lush landscape. Amber haze waned on the horizon. Thomas put his right hand over his head and watched the sun descend behind an old rock wall. The edges glowed the exact same color as his ring.

"So the sun sets here as well," Thomas said.

"The sun sets on everything, even Ungland," Kuzen replied.

"What is Ungland? I mean, where is it and what is it like?"

The first twinkle of starlight glistened overhead. Two large blimps flew by. A still-image of Hillary's face hung between the wires dangling from the blimps. Her cold blue eyes seemed to watch Thomas and Kuzen as they vanished beneath the blimp's pitch-black shadow.

"Look Thomas, I know I've put this off for far too long, but we have to put it off longer still. We need to make an ally of Germany or Poland. Having both would be best, but they aren't likely to work together."

"You're changing the subject," Thomas said while crossing his arms.

Kuzen removed his black, wide-brimmed hat and stuck it under his left armpit.

"We'll arrive in Ungland after passing through Poland. I could tell you about your homeland, your parents, and even yourself. However, that would color your memories with my interpretation. I would gloss over the painful details and obscure the things I don't want you to know."

Thomas uncrossed his arms and held them at his sides.

"Kuzen, just who exactly are you. And why are you helping me?" Thomas asked.

Cold wind blew across the plain. Kuzen's remaining hairs stood up on end.

"I am nobody today. You will remember yourself soon. The sight of Ungland will guarantee that. What you remember of me and how you react to that memory will determine if I am to remain a nobody for the remainder of my life."

"What do you mean?"

Kuzen replaced his hat on his head and pulled the brim over his eyes. Whether he meant to respond or not, circumstances denied him the chance. A faded green wagon approached from across the plains. The driver, two elderly men, a woman, and boy waved to Thomas and Kuzen. The driver came to a stop with a dramatic turn. Hot exhaust settled around the two Unglish men.

The driver, a teenager with a shaved head and bruised eyes, leaned out of his window and said, "Fahren Sie mit uns in die Stadt. Die Amerikaner können jederzeit angreifen und du bist in diesem Bereich anfällig."

"You understand a word of that?" Kuzen asked.

Thomas tried to think back to his childhood.

"I remember a plain white classroom and a shriveled up teaching lady that smelled of piss. I remember chemistry lessons with a cross-eyed classmate and French classes by the beach. Nothing about your identity or mine comes to mind. And there's not a single word of German to be found," Thomas replied.

A forty-something, blonde woman sat in the front passenger seat.

While Kuzen talked to Thomas, she leaned near the driver and whispered, "Sie klingen amerikanisch."

When Thomas replied, the driver nodded his head and exited the wagon.

"Gehen Sie nach Hause," he said while slamming his fist against the wagon's hood.

Two elderly men stepped from the driver's side back seat and closed in on the Unglanders. One carried a gardening hoe; the other held an iron baseball bat.

"Don't make me sauer your kraut," Kuzen barked while arming the spring in his artificial heel.

Thomas removed his jacket and held up his fists. As the driver swung wide, over Thomas's right shoulder, Thomas ducked to the left and drove his right arm into the driver's stomach. The driver fell backwards and the two passengers rushed past him. One old man swung the garden hoe at Thomas's head. Clumps of hair hung in the wind as Thomas dodged just in time. Kuzen leapt past Thomas and kicked the hoe-wielding German into his baseball-bat wielding companion. The three Germans lay on the ground, looking upwards and clutching their chests.

"Should we take their car?" Kuzen asked.

The woman and boy rolled up their windows. Thomas stood over the driver and as blood trickled from a scratch on his crown. Shadows eclipsed all. A medium sized blimp passed overhead, projecting an image of Thomas's face on the side. The message "Kill this man to end the war" appeared intermittently at the bottom in English, French, German, and Polish text.

Kuzen put his hand to his forehead and looked at the wide-open landscape ahead.

"We'll never win the Germans to our side at this rate," he said.

Thomas shook his head then reached out his hand. Though they had no method of speaking to each other, the strangers understood each-others intent. The driver took Thomas's hand and stood. He confiscated his passenger's weapons and flung them into the underbrush. The remaining two passengers rolled down their windows and unlocked their doors. Thomas, Kuzen, and the Germans climbed inside. The drive was initially silent. Germans stole glances at Thomas the entire way.

"Think they're planning on turning us in?" Kuzen asked.

"No," Thomas replied. "They're taking us to Germany's deposed king."

Kuzen pulled the brim of his hat over his eyes and looked down at his belt buckle.

"That isn't possible Thomas."

"Why?"

Kuzen and Thomas sat in the third row from the front of the wagon. The two elderly men sat in the second row. The driver and middle-aged blonde woman sat in the first while a young boy slept restlessly in the hatch. Kuzen glanced at each of the passengers before replying.

"When the current Chancellor of Germany, Havana Gila, stole power,"

"Wait, the same Gila we just escaped from," Thomas interrupted.

"The one and only. When he stole power from your Great Uncle Jim."

"Wait, Jim?"

"Yes, Jim."

"Just Jim?"

"Well no, his full name is Jim Limpdickfaggotballs the Third."

Thomas threw up his hands and lamented, "Let's just call him Jim."

"As I was saying, Havana Gila didn't just depose your uncle Jim, he had him beheaded!"

"Wait, as in head chopped off?" Thomas asked.

"I guess you could look at it as having his body chopped off. Havana Gila is a radical Jew."

"He rides a skate board with yarmulkes for wheels?"

"That's very cute Thomas. Can I get back to expositing now? Its kind of what I do."

"Sure."

Kuzen cracked his back, then continued speaking.

"Gila took this country by force and rules it with an iron fist. Back to the point though, Jim had no heirs. The Limpdickfaggotballs family is gone forever."

"Zat is not exactly true," a deep, yet feminine voice rasped.

"Ah, so you sprechen sie deutsch after all," Kuzen said.

"Of course I sprechen sie deutsch, that means speak the German you buffoon," the woman in the front passenger seat replied.

Kuzen pulled his cap brim further down his brow. He pulled so hard in fact, that his hat popped clean off his head and landed in his lap.

"Oh, I do love a balding man," The blonde said under her breath.

Kuzen caught his cap after fumbling with it twice and pulled it tightly over his brow.

"You were saying, frawliney?" Kuzen said.

"It's pronounced fraulein you silly person. And as I was saying, the previous chancellor was of the ancient bloodline. As I can see from the glowing red ring on your finger young man, you too are of zat bloodline."

Thomas looked down at his right hand. His blood red ring gleamed menacingly in the darkness.

"So you know that old royals can withstand heat, what does that have to do with my murdered uncle?" Thomas asked.

The German woman turned around fully as she spoke. Her flaxen hair fell across the head of her seat. Were the two old men seated behind her awake, they would have had ample opportunity to ogle her large, somewhat sagging breasts. Kuzen was only half-awake himself but inadvertently took the opportunity. Thomas kept his gaze upon his father's ring.

"As you may or not know, young man. Each branch of the royal family has their own special gift, or curse, depending on whom you ask. This uncle of yours was a Limpdickfaggotballs; therefore he was also gifted or cursed in a certain way," she said while staring into Kuzen's eyes.

He looked up, caught her gaze, and jerked his neck to the right in order to look out of his window.

"What do you mean in a certain way?" Thomas asked.

The blonde turned to her immediate right and whispered into the driver's ear, "Fahren Sie uns zum Versteck. Diese beiden haben das Geschäft mit dem Huthalter."

The driver took a hard turn to the left and sped towards

his new destination. The German woman glanced at our heroes and smiled.

"We are taking the two of you to meet an important friend. You have two hours to sleep. I suggest you use them," she said.

Her eyes lingered on Kuzen. Kuzen swallowed hard and pretended not to notice. Thomas leaned against the car door to his left and fell immediately to sleep.

"You have a thing for blondes don't you young man?" the woman asked.

"Yeah, and it's about the size of a loaf of bread," he said with a wink.

"I'll have to show you my bread box later," she replied.

Kuzen swallowed saliva and peered outside of his window. Small, lightless towns peppered the landscape.

"Have the Jews really taken over?" he asked.

"Yes, Havana stormed the Chancellor's manor and demanded his head. Jim could have resisted easily if not for one thing, his guilt."

"Guilt?" Kuzen asked.

"Yes, you'll find out why later, but Jim kneeled before Havana Gila and offered his head. The Jews for the most part are benign, so long as we don't disturb their prayers or leaven our bread. But every now and again, Havana picks a town and a piece of Talmudic law that they have inadvertently violated. He then rounds up the men, women, children, house pets, and even the transsexuals and cuts off their heads."

Kuzen blinked three times and took a sudden breath.

"You really should rest now. That prince seems a hefty burden to carry," she said.

"Trust me," Kuzen replied. "Thomas is the one carrying me,"

"Oh, so zat is the young man's name," she said while pressing her breasts against the head of her chair.

"Yes, and you'll have to excuse my rudeness for not introducing myself before. My name is Kuzen."

"So neither of you have last names?"

"As far as you are concerned, we don't," Kuzen said while narrowing his eyes.

"Ok, ok, I understand. You ooze charm like a retard oozes genetic futility into the front of his sonic the hedgehog underoos, so I'll let this go. My name is Künstliche Fische. If you would like, I can join you back there Kazoo," Künstliche said while licking her dry red lips.

"That's Kuzen. And for now I'd rather sleep," Kuzen replied while pulling his wide brimmed hat over his eyes.

Sleep came quickly. Kuzen suffered a reoccurring dream and awoke clutching his false leg. Thomas slumbered quietly next to Kuzen. The wagon was otherwise empty. Inky blackness permeated their windows. A swaying canopy of ancient trees kept any particle of light from reaching their wagon. Kuzen leaned in close to Thomas and shook him gently by the shoulder.

"Wake up, and hold your tongue. The Germs are up to

something," he whispered.

Thomas roused slowly, then studied Kuzen with half-shut eyes. He heard footsteps behind him and peered outside his window. He put his right hand upon the glass. Beyond the red gleam of his burning ring, a bloated, decapitated head watched Thomas with bulging, bloodshot eyes.

11.

Our heroes recoiled. Doors swung open. Kuzen tumbled outside. As Kuzen scrambled to his feet, the head closed in on Thomas. Its cracked blue tongue flailed silently in the dark.

"Please wait," Künstliche said while sliding between Kuzen and the wagon. "He wanted to meet the deposed chancellor, and now he shall. Besides, you and I have business of our own to attend."

She smirked and gestured towards a distant tent.

Kuzen glanced over his shoulder and said, "Eh, he'll probably be fine."

The gibbering head rested atop a silver plate. Its left eye watched Thomas. The right eye drooped over its cheekbone. A deep inhalation sounded, followed by a quiet hiss that lasted for several seconds. Wind sent treetops in motion. Moonlight revealed the woman who carried the head. She held the plate with one hand. With the other, she worked an accordion shaped air pump against her thigh. Once the leather bladder connected to the pump was full, the assistant connected it to the underside of the silver plate. The decapitated head's eyes sunk back into place as it opened its mouth to speak.

"You came all this way, just for a little head?" It asked in a wispy voice. "That was only a joke my boy. Others joke about my physique all the time and I try to keep ahead of them. Get it? A head!"

The assistant placed her hands over the head's rotting ears.

"Don't pay his puns any mind," she said. "His brains are slowly turning into mush."

Her honey colored eyes seemed almost luminescent in the dark. Suddenly, Thomas envied the head that rested on her lap.

"As I was saying," the head continued. "My son claims you are a relative of mine. Tell me Thomas, from whence have you come, and perhaps, have you brought me a hat? The nights are long since we've been in hiding and I fear I'm coming down with a head cold."

Thomas grimaced, then replied, "I know neither my past nor lineage. I am told that I am the rightful heir to the Unglish throne, though I know nothing of that country. And as far as your son is concerned, I don't believe we've met."

"Didn't you notice him in the wagon? He has long blonde hair, big breasts, and an ass that won't quit."

"You don't mean…"

"Yes he, or perhaps she, as she keeps reminding me to say, is my child. Künstliche was born to a pigeon-toed Polack prostitute near the end of the second world war. While I fought on the front lines, she filled our child's heart with hate. I never thought of the Nazis or their ideals. I only knew that the Russians were coming to kill us. If only I had been so fortunate. I spent so many years as a prisoner of war, that I eventually forgot the color of the sun. Upon release, I went in search of my son. Like me, he was a broken man that could find no quarter. Swastika tattoos covered his skin, projecting the shame of our nation's past. He begged me to take him in, but I wouldn't listen. I told Künstliche that we would be strangers until he cut the cursed skin from his body. We met again in a hospital ten years ago when he took me up on my offer. His body was so shredded and ruined, if not for our curse, he would have never survived."

"And is that why he had a sex change? Because he ruined

his um, you know."

"No, Künstliche had no problems down there. He elected for the implants because he's the kinky son of a syphilitic Polish whore."

"Oh."

Thomas glanced towards Künstliche's tent. The poles bent inwards and the canvas rustled with motion. He wondered how Kuzen would react to his upcoming surprise.

"Are you ashamed of him?"

"I was for the longest time," the head replied. "We Limpdickfaggotballs can live forever so long as our brains are left intact. In addition, once we reach our forties, we cease to age. For decades, I could not understand how my son could bare his shameful past. These last few years I have spent with him, or her, watching her gather and organize our people, I have come to love her for the first time since she was an infant."

The assistant wiped a tear from her beautiful eyes. In doing so, she nearly dropped the silver plate.

"I swear I'd loose my head if it wasn't attached," she remarked.

The head rolled its sunken eyes and continued, "Too long have my people bent beneath this yolk of shame. Were your father Richard here, I am certain he would urge me to not only defeat Havana, but Hillary as well."

"Can you tell me about my father?" Thomas asked.

The head attempted to shake from side to side.

"You must focus on the road ahead, Thomas. You cannot go back. Looking back won't help you either."

Thomas slid across his seat and grasped the plate. The head assistant meant to intervene, but brushed against Thomas's ring and recoiled.

"Why mustn't I know? Why is everyone keeping things from me?" Thomas pleaded.

The head tried to respond, but its air bladder proved empty. The assistant hurried to fill it with her accordion pump.

"You will learn all you need to know upon reaching your father's throne room," it continued once the air bladder was full. "It is imperative that you do so. I can retake my country without you, but we have no chance of staving off the Americans without the support of Ungland."

Thomas studied his ring and tried to remember his father. Nothing came to mind.

"How do you mean to retake Germany?" he asked after some time.

"Oh, it is simple really. Anybody could do it," the assistant interrupted.

The head grimaced. The assistant covered her mouth and pretended to look out of her window.

"Havana Gila took power alone. His followers poured into the country later on. As of this night, he has just twenty five men loyal to his cause."

"Twenty five Jews conquered Germany! How?" Thomas asked in a raised voice.

"When the Jews came to take our land, we feared being labeled as anti-Semitic too much to resist them. Long I have sat on this plate, unwilling to stand on my own two feet. Now that the Americans are at our doorstep, I have no choice but to act. As we speak, a group of German rebels is drawing Havana Gila and his disciples to the German-Polish boarder. When your escort is ready, we shall fly to meet them. I mean fly as a figure of speech of course. Our means are meager and I've misplaced my propeller beanie cap."

The head paused for Thomas to laugh but Thomas felt little of the intended humor.

"Then what are we waiting for?" Thomas asked.

Pinpoints of candle light appeared behind the wagon. Four German men in thick black cloaks opened the hatch and stored a large wooden crate inside. Before leaving, one of those men tossed a crumpled sock cap to the head assistant.

She placed it atop the head and asked, "Could you go get your friend, Thomas?"

Before Thomas could exit the wagon, Kuzen stormed out of the tent and ran to Thomas's door.

"Let me in," he barked.

"How was it?" Thomas asked.

"It was dark."

"I'm not asking about the lighting."

"I said it was dark!" Kuzen yelled as he forced his way inside.

He pushed Thomas into the middle-most seat and pulled his hat over his face.

"That's a very nice cap," The head whispered to his assistant. "But I believe I've seen it someplace before."

"Shut up before I mount you on a cabin wall," Kuzen growled.

Thomas and the assistant laughed. The head meant to laugh with them but was completely out of air. Künstliche exited her tent in a beautiful yellow dress. Her long blonde hair caught the wind like a gossamer sail. She then pulled a wedgie loose and hobbled towards the wagon.

"Looks like she got the wurst of your brat," Thomas whispered with a grin.

Kuzen elbowed Thomas in the ribs. The drive to the Polish border passed silently. Künstliche and a rifle-toting driver sat in the two front seats. Everyone else slept in the back. While dozing, Thomas inadvertently slumped against the head assistant's breasts. He listened to the rhythmic beating of her heart and tried to place his hand upon her thigh. The head awoke and bit Thomas's hand.
"I could toss you from the window right now," Thomas whispered.

"I'd scream my head off," the head replied.

Thomas crossed his arms, then slept the for remainder of the drive. The land between Poland and Germany was expansive and undeveloped. Twenty-six men stood on one side of an old stone wall. Dozens more stood their ground on the opposite side. Behind them, dozens of military vehicles idled ominously.

"Are those tanks with us?" Thomas asked.

"Those forces belong to the Polish border patrol," the head assistant replied.

Thomas meant to pursue small talk, but a low flying blimp passed overhead and its speakers blared, "The English and French have fallen. Give us the prince or face our wrath!"

Kuzen and Künstliche exited the wagon. The driver waved them off, then fell to sleep in his seat. As Thomas helped the head assistant step outside, the plate trembled between her fingers.

"Eat these," Künstliche said while tossing sausages to our heroes.

"Why now?" Thomas asked.

"You can't shit your pants on an empty stomach," Kuzen replied while biting into his wiener.

"When you boys are done playing with your sausages, I'll need a little help handling my box," Künstliche said with a smirk.

Thomas raised an eyebrow. Kuzen gagged.

As Künstliche opened the hatch, she whispered, "You're an expert on handling back-doors, aren't you?" into Kuzen's ear.

Kuzen grumbled and pulled the long wooden box from the hatch in a single jerk.

"Careful, mein friends!" the head cried as the foot end of the box struck soil.

Kuzen knelt. Thomas grasped the other end. Though the box was heavy, they made steady progress towards the border. Künstliche stood in front and swayed her hips every step of the way. Kuzen bit his lip and tried to keep his morning sausage down.

"Hello young prince!" Havana cried as our heroes approached. "How kind of you to surrender and keep our wonderful allies from killing us all. We must thank them, yes we must."

He pulled a curved sword from his beard and pointed it at Thomas. The decapitated head gulped. Saliva trickled down his remaining portion of throat and sullied his plate.

"That's the sword-" He began.

"Yes, I circumcised your entire head with this blade two years ago. Now I'll use it to carve kosher meat from our rebel prince!" Havana interrupted.

A woman in a large black robe ran out of a forest and stood next to Havana. Her hairless scalp glistened in the sun. White cloth obscured a dark facial bruise, which, as we all know, is the second most satisfying type of facial you can give a woman. A wriggling newborn wept in her shaking hands.

"Please, the Americans are coming," she said. "I don't want my bubby to die with his foreskin intact!"

Havana took the child in his wrinkled fingers. The babe cooed. Havana bit through the baby's penis. He chewed it in the left side of his mouth twice before spitting it in the mother's face. She grasped her baby and recoiled in horror.

"You're a monster!" she cried.

"Expect an invoice," Havana replied.

Thomas and Kuzen set down the long wooden crate. Künstliche and the head assistant broke it open as the men prepared to fight.

"It's not too late to convert and die as one of God's chosen people. Just kidding. Jews only accept converts with leverageable power," Havana said while twirling his blade.

Though his sword moved around his body at a tremendous speed, he did not cut a single hair from his beard.

"You are a sad little man," Thomas replied.

"Is that all you have to say?" Havana asked.

"No, you're beard stinks too," Kuzen added while arming the spring in his heel.

"Nobody insults my stinky beard!" Havana screamed while charging forward.

Twenty-five disciples pulled daggers from their cloaks. Dozens of Germans hopped the stone wall to intercept them.

"Haven't you Nazis done my people enough harm?" Havana asked loudly in German, causing the soldiers to falter.

"Have none of you a working functioning pair of balls?" Kuzen asked.

Künstliche slowly raise her hand. The others hung their heads in shame.

"One man is no more his people than his descendant the

bearer of his sin," Thomas rasped.

Künstliche shouted Thomas's words in German. The soldiers nodded, then intercepted the disciples. Icy metal danced over Thomas's crown. He ducked and grasped Havana's beard. Kuzen's right arm slipped over Thomas's left shoulder and slammed Havana in the nose. He then recoiled and shook his fractured hand. Havana sliced at Thomas vertically and cut his own beard in twain. He stepped backwards and clutched at the missing patch.

"Aren't you ashamed?" he asked. "Don't you know what those filthy German's did to my people? Didn't you learn from television how they enslaved seventeen million innocent Jews? They killed twenty five million Jews! That's thirty three million murdered people. And not just any people, but God's chosen people!" He pointed a knobby finger at Künstliche and screamed, "And you, weren't you a skinhead! Why would you join such a terrible group of people?"

Künstliche looked directly into Havana's eyes. A cloud passed over the sun. The only remaining sliver of light connected her to Havana.

"I was young and simple minded. My mother told me zat a terrible thing was good and I believed her," Künstliche said.

"And I'm supposed to believe that?" Havana screamed while shaking his sword.

Künstliche smiled and added, "Well, it seemed like the thing to do at the time. I mean, all the popular kids were doing it and it beat the hell out of yodeling."

Havana stepped forward and grumbled, "I'll be especially particular in the means of your execution."

"Never again!" the decapitated head screamed.

A loud knock sounded between Künstliche and the head assistant. A bloated body in a bloodied, green suit stood from the wooden crate. It reached towards the head assistant, who handed over the head and took a step backwards. Jim Limpdickfaggotballs grasped his head and put it firmly back onto his shoulders. He cracked his neck from left to right, then from the front to the back.

"We Germans must not and can not continue to toil beneath the shadows of deluded grandfathers and advantage seeking men such as you," he said in a booming voice.

He pushed Thomas and Kuzen aside so that he and Havana stood one sword stroke apart.

"I let you take my head once out of self hatred and shame."

He looked back at his daughter and smiled, then turned towards Havana and continued to speak,

"But now I see that we Germans can come back from our past and grasp of our future, with our own hands!"

"Du sagst ihm, Papa!" Künstliche screamed.

"The only thing for you to grasp is the lid of your coffin," Havana growled while lunging forward.

Jim made a head butting motion that sent his head flying forward. It passed mere nanometers above Havana's blade and struck Havana in the forehead. Havana stumbled backwards and flailed his sword wildly. After seven swings, he stopped to catch his breath. Blood ran down his sword. The headless body kneeled to retrieve its head. It then stood and fixed the head in place. Jim attempted to speak, but his head was slightly crooked and his words came out as gurgled.

"Künstliche!" he called after twisting his head on straight.

Künstliche ran to her father's side. Jim placed his arm on his daughter's shoulder and smiled.

"Künstliche, though this man will not forgive us; I forgive him and all of his people. Hatred waylays them as strongly as I was misled by shame. In my weakness, I allowed you to suffer. Please, my child. Can you forgive me?" he asked.

Künstliche wrapped her arms around her father and squeezed. Jim's head nearly fell off mid hug but Künstliche pushed it back into place.

"Don't think for a moment this is over!" Havana screamed.

Blood poured into his mouth as he spoke. He grasped his face in surprise.

"You blind fool," Künstliche said. "In your barrage of blades you've bisected the biggest and bittiest bits from your body."

Peering down, Havana saw that the end of his nose and his entire penis lay in a puddle of blood. He dropped his sword and fell to his knees.

"Serves you right!" a female voice screamed.

The Jewish mother ran towards Havana and shoved him to the ground. She scooped up Havana's mangled penis and tossed it into her gown. She then stopped in front of Jim and bowed.

"My son might not be circumcised by a Jew, but thanks to you, and a very reasonably priced surgery, he'll have twice as many peckers as anyone!" she said before scurrying away.

Havana grasped the end of his nose. As he tried to attach it to his bleeding crotch, blood poured through the nostrils.

"That's one hell of a botched nose job," Kuzen said.

Thomas and the Limpdickfaggotballs laughed. The head assistant bent over and vomited strudel on the back of Thomas's shoes.

"You're nothing but a Havana Gila-monster!" Jim said.

Only Jim and Künstliche laughed. They laughed and held each other as though for the first time in ages.

"Germans!" Jim commanded in German. "Dispel these disciples from our land!"

The three dozen German men and women disarmed the disciples and allowed them to stand. They gathered around Havana and walked towards the Polish border.

"Should we try to ally with the Poles?" one of them asked.

"No," Havana replied. "The one in the black suit popped me right in the face. I'll get his ass later in a civil suit. Stupid goy!"

Thomas and his newfound friends meant to celebrate. The head assistant hugged Thomas. Künstliche caught Kuzen by surprise and grabbed his ass with both hands. Jim was the first to hear the fluttering sound. He turned back so fast that his body turned but his head stayed in place. He twisted his neck around and nearly fell over in surprise. Twenty red, white, and blue helicopters flew over the forests. Dozens of wheelchair bound Americans rolled towards them from the tree line.

Jim took Künstliche by both hands and pleaded, "You must rally our troops, Künstliche. I had my chance to lead our people and allowed the power to go to my head. Now that task falls upon you."

Künstliche nodded and kissed her father's forehead.

"But what will you do?" she asked.

"Our prince needs an escort to Poland and I suspect an immortal should suffice."

He shoved Künstliche and the head assistant towards the wagon. Künstliche stole glances at Kuzen as he ran towards the border with Thomas and her father. As her wagon pulled away, she could have sworn she saw him look back.

12.

Thomas, Jim, and Kuzen sprinted towards the border while American troops rolled after them and shredded trees with their armrest-mounted M16s. One American mistook a grenade in his cup-holder for a beer and pulled the tab. His immense bulk of half-cooked man flesh flew throughout the forest. A slab of back fat struck Kuzen's false leg and bent it in half. Thomas and Jim took Kuzen by the shoulders and continued sprinting. Two thirds of the pursuing Americans slowed to a crawl beneath the hail of meat. They slumped out of their chairs and began to consume their fallen comrade. One American ate so much that his one-size-fits-all uniform split down the middle. He rolled downhill while reaching for a chocolate bar he kept in his top most gut fold and inadvertently inserted his thumb into the anus of a fellow soldier. She was an elderly black woman with a lovely smile and tits the size of refrigerators. A slab of fat landed on her shirt and she tore into it like a complimentary buffet. She turned around and smiled. Suddenly, she and the first soldier began making love. Other soldiers crawled out of their chairs and rolled downhill for an impromptu orgy. Someone pulled a stick of butter from their fanny pack and dispersed it for use as personal lubrication. Thomas looked back and wretched. Kuzen tended to his prosthetic leg. Jim watched the throbbing mass of American bodies and placed his head at crotch level in order to hide his erection.

"I really wasn't expecting that," Jim remarked.

"I am not particularly surprised," Thomas replied.

"Now is not the time for small talk," Kuzen said as he snapped his leg back into place.

He pointed to a red helicopter that hovered overhead. A morbidly obese man struggled to squeeze into the side mounted gun pod.

"Meine mutter's mustache, he's going to shoot!" Jim screamed.

He jumped in front of Thomas and absorbed two high impact bullets with his chest. The gunman would have continued firing, but his ample gut caught in the firing mechanism. He grit his teeth and tried to pull away. A strip of man bacon tore from his torso and flapped in the air like a meaty flag.

"My precious body mass!" he screamed while grasping and tearing into his own strip of flesh.

A second soldier waddled over and fought the gunner for the tumor-laden treat. The unbearable weight of two Americans on one side of the helicopter caused it to tip sideways and crash. Thomas and Kuzen sprinted to outrun the explosion. Jim lagged behind in order to absorb the spray of shrapnel that followed. As our heroes stood only three paces from the border, Jim backed away. He eyed the orgy in the distance and licked his purple lips.

"Here we part ways, young prince," he said while plucking a shard of metal from his thigh. "I will penetrate their line and keep the Americans from coming as long as possible. If they slip behind us, I will personally back into them and act as an absorbent blanket."

"Whatever," Kuzen grunted as Jim sprinted away.

"Which way to now?" Thomas asked.

Kuzen pointed towards a mountain in the distance. Five tanks and three jeeps stood in their way. A tank aimed at Thomas and fired. The shell landed at his feet but did not explode. The other four tanks remained perfectly still.

"We'll never make it," Thomas lamented.

"We'll be fine," Kuzen replied.

He leaned over the shell and removed the top, then poured the contents of the long end into the top like a cup and held it beneath his nose.

"This is the Polish army we're dealing with," he continued while gently gyrating the lid in his hand.

He held it to his lips and took a sip.

"Half of those tanks are cardboard. And this shell is actually a thermos full of red beet soup. Just follow my lead and we'll make it to that mountain fine."

He handed the cup to Thomas. It was warm to the touch and smelled pleasantly sweet. Thomas raised the cup to his lips as the polish tank fired a second volley. The shell landed wide right and destroyed a patch of trees. Searing embers fell across their shoulders.

"On second thought, cheese it!" Kuzen screamed.

A jeep burst through the treeline, turned hard right, rolled three times, then landed on it's wheels inches from our heroes. The driver slumped out of his seat and stumble towards Thomas.

"That blimp said to kill you to end the war and I always do what blimps tell me. Which is why I always have a good year! Are you ready to taste cold steel?" the Polish soldier rasped while drawing his pistol.

"Ooh, do me first!" Kuzen replied before opening his mouth wide.

"You want me to shoot you?"

"Sure thing pal, Bullets taste like candy."

"Like candy?"

"Like candy wrapped in smelly fermented cabbage," Thomas added.

"Wowee!"

As the Polish soldier placed the pistol in his mouth, Kuzen and Thomas hopped into the idling jeep. Blood spattered the back window as they pulled away. Thomas headed for the mountain in the distance. Its peak penetrated the clouds. Its stony grey face seemed an impenetrable barrier.

"Can we really cross that mountain?" Thomas asked while pointing ahead.

Kuzen put his feet on the dash and nodded.

"It's been done before."

He pulled his hat over his face and said no more.

"Pull over or we'll shoot!" a voice crackled via the jeeps radio.

A helicopter followed them closely. The gunner kept his sights trained on Thomas's head. Thomas forced the jeep to a stop. A loud crack followed and Thomas checked his body for a bullet hole. He looked to his right and saw Kuzen struggling to pull his leg from the broken windshield.

"What the hell?" Kuzen asked.

"Haven't you been paying attention?" Thomas replied.

Kuzen adjusted his hat, then reached for the console mounted mouthpiece.

"Aren't you cold?" he asked.

"Well, yes, I am," the pilot replied.

"It's because of that pesky fan over your head."

"Of course, why didn't I think of that?"

"Drive!" Kuzen yelped.

Thomas stomped onto the gas just in time to avoid the crashing copter. Fire and shrapnel rained upon the roof. They reached the base of the mountain twenty minutes later. Thomas opened the driver's side door but remained in his seat. Kuzen exited the jeep and hobbled around to Thomas's window.

"Can we really climb it?" Thomas asked.

"It's been done before."

Kuzen coughed and quietly undid the top button of his undershirt.

"Thirsty, aren't you?" Thomas said.

"There's plenty to drink on the other side," Kuzen replied.

He then removed his false leg and broke it over his artificial knee.

"What the hell did you do that for?" Thomas asked.

He stepped out of the jeep and bent over the broken halves of Kuzen's leg.

"That prosthetic weighs twenty one pounds and suits our purposes better broken," Kuzen replied.

He bent slowly and grasped one-half of his prosthetic leg, then made a stabbing motion with it while peering up at Thomas.

"One good stab is all it takes to establish a hold on the rock. This mountain looks tall, and it is tall. However, the path we're to take is relatively gradual and the rock is porous. I know you can do this Thomas. If I didn't believe in you, I wouldn't have brought you all this way."

Kuzen hopped to the mountainside and ran his hands across it, then grasped the ankle of his ruined false leg and drove the metal tibia into the mountain. He hoisted himself into the air with his free hand and found a foothold with his natural left leg. He drove the metallic shaft into the mountainside again and climbed another arms length upward. Once he repeated the process thrice, Thomas followed behind him. Several times, Kuzen changed directions. Sometimes he went up, sometimes left and right, twice he even descended. Thomas searched the mountainside for their destination. Nothing obvious came into view.

"Hurry up!" Kuzen called out about forty minutes into the climb.

Thomas glanced up and saw Kuzen peering down at him from a ledge. A loud rumble sounded behind Thomas. He looked back and watched fifty grey blimps slip across the Polish sky. From their position in relation to the sun, they resembled pitch-black titans on march for Ungland.

"Have they come to deliver another message?" Thomas asked while hurrying upwards.

"No. That is an escort. We cannot see it now. But there is probably a special aircraft in the center."

"Who do you think is piloting it?" Thomas asked.

Kuzen did not reply. He frowned, grasped the back of Thomas's brown suit, and swiftly hoisted Thomas onto the ledge. They stood before a five-foot tall and two-foot wide crack in the side of the mountain. Kuzen removed his hat, placed it inside his jacket, and buttoned his jacket completely.

"There are many branching paths within," he said. "Only one leads to Ungland. The others drop suddenly towards oblivion. On top of that, we won't be entirely alone."

Thomas meant to replied, but low-pitched, echoing laughter cut him off as they entered the cave. Thomas hurried forward and placed his hand on Kuzen's back.

"Please don't," Kuzen said. "I'm off balance enough as it is. You're well enough to stand on your own."

"Ok Kuzen. Take your time".

"Sorry, no time for taking time."

Kuzen dropped his half of his broken prosthetic and hurried forward. Tiny insects fluttered throughout the cave. Thomas could not see them, but they turned out in droves to fly into his face.

"Can't we do anything about these bugs?" Thomas asked.

"If we stop running into them, we'll know we've gone the wrong way,"

Thomas meant to reply. However, a large luminescent moth flew into his mouth and he spat it onto Kuzen's back. Blue flames singed Kuzen's suit from the edge of strange moth's wings. The dim blue glow let Thomas know he was not too far behind.

"So who was that laughing?" Thomas whispered.

"The Mad King roams these halls."

"But I thought I was king?"

"You are, of Ungland. We trespass now among the bones of the mountain. It's King watches, waiting for a chance to strike."

"Will we be alright?"

"Probably not," an aged, yet powerful voice echoed from every direction.

Thomas felt a change in the air and cried for Kuzen to turn back. Kuzen's screams echoed down a fifteen hundred foot drop. Thomas reached out and grasped Kuzen by the back of his jacket. The luminescent moth flew between Thomas's fingers and landed on his burning ring as Thomas pulled with all his might. Kuzen thrashed his arms in a circular motion. The buttons on his shirt broke and his hat fell free. Thomas gave one last pull; the last he would have been able to manage. Kuzen caught his hat on his remaining foot and fell backwards onto Thomas's stomach.

"I thought you knew the way," Thomas said between gasping breaths.

"The last time I roamed these halls I dragged a ruined leg behind me," Kuzen replied. He placed his hat atop his head and added, "It's harder to follow my trail of blood than I expected."

"It's never so easy," the powerful voice replied.

Thomas turned back, led the way towards the erroneous turn, and veered left at the fork. They passed through a narrow, winding hallway. The further they crept, the louder the powerful voice seemed.

"Let me tell you a story," the voice began.

"We're too old for bed time stories!" Kuzen replied.

The voice chuckled, then continued, "There was once a king beneath this mountain with two beloved brothers and a sister. That king was powerful, and all feared his wrath. However, the nearness of his family left him ill at ease. The strongest brother could usurp him by the might of his hand. The handsome brother could charm diplomats into sabotaging the king. Even the intelligent sister could trick him into destruction! One day, this king beneath the trembling stone called his family, one at a time, into the chambers you now approach. The strongest brother approached the throne, clutching a tremendous hammer. He fell into a cleverly laid shaft that would only break beneath his considerable weight as he hefted his hammer for a blow. His crumpled remains were then retrieved and roasted on a skewer."

Thomas grimaced. Kuzen balled his left hand into a fist.

"The handsome brother walked in on the king's familial feast and began to scream. Oh, how that King laughed. His laughter filled the royal halls, changing them into dank passageways. The handsome brother called for guards and diplomats to help him. A boulder, pushed by a man cuckolded by the prince, fell from a hidden ledge and smote the handsome brother. Guards compelled him towards a boiling pot. He resisted until he perceived his ruined visage reflected in the bubbling waters. The younger sister, oh how precious she once was. She wept when she saw her brothers boiling in the pot and roasted on the king's plate. 'Don't be such a crybaby', the ugly brother whimpered while seasoning himself. This sister meant to use her wits against the king, a blasphemous action that was. However, emotion clouded her judgment. The king offered her reprieve if she would only kiss his hand. She grasped a knife from the table as she approached. The king smiled and shoved her back. That sister, once so intelligent and lovely fell upon her own blade. She was eaten raw.

"Why are you telling us this?" Thomas asked.

"Those that use strength without thought, charm without restraint, or intelligence without fortitude may not pass beneath this mountain. I have met once, the force that follows you. It spoke of the evils of strength, beauty, and intelligence without a syllable spoken of their good. Perhaps you should be allowed to escape only to defy that force."

A particle of light illuminated the path ahead.

"Do you see that?" Thomas asked while running forward.

"Wait!" Kuzen screamed.

Thomas ignored Kuzen's warning. What appeared to be a beam of light shining from a distant path proved to be a horizontal cut in the mountain wall. Thomas slammed into it a full speed. The wall gave way as if hinge swung open. Golden light poured inside the hallway. Thousands of insects flew past Kuzen into the remaining darkness. Kuzen fell to his knees and peered down the side of the mountain. Jagged rocks stuck out in regular intervals directly below. Golden light draped downwards and struck a silvery sea. Warm ocean spray danced between fang-shaped rocks at the base of the mountain. Kuzen held the back of his hand to his forehead and collapsed.

"Everything for nothing. Now I can never take it back," he said while wringing his hat between his fingers.

"I'm not sure what you're getting at, but if it isn't terribly important we should probably save it for later," a familiar voice replied.

Kuzen looked to his immediate left. The top of Kuzen's prosthetic leg protruded from a crack in the mountainside door. Thomas held on with one hand. His feet dangled in the warm Unglish air. Kuzen doubled over and laughed so hard, he thought his lungs would burst. Thomas meant to ask for help, but Kuzen's laughter was so joyful and genuine that Thomas could not help but laugh with him. Kuzen stood finally and pulled Thomas onto the side of the mountain. He then swung his left leg over the side, found a foothold and took the first step down. Thomas reached for the remaining half of Kuzen's false leg.

"Leave it," Kuzen said. "It makes a better doorknob than a leg at this point."

The mountain door slowly closed as Thomas and Kuzen descended. A strange smile glimmered in the dark. Crawling down proved a great deal easier than climbing up. Ten minutes into their descent, Thomas and Kuzen rested atop a flat rock halfway down the mountain. Thomas looked up from his blistered hands and saw Ungland in all its glory. Two hundred feet of silvery water stood between them and the sovereign nation. The mountain on which they sat wrapped around Ungland and its waters in a perfect circle with a diameter of five miles. The country of Ungland itself was a circle of land only three-miles in diameter. Tall white buildings stuck out from the silver sea. Golden tipped spires, painted red and green, reflected prisms of light across the sky. Irregularly shaped buildings with grand arches and tiny black windows stuck out of the sea. Unglanders swam between the buildings. Vendors peddled their wears on ornate canoes. Flowers and budding fruits hung from vines on the sides of every building.

"What a beautiful land," Thomas said.

He felt a vein throb in the back of his head, as though a memory wanted to break free but was unable to.

"It should be. You and your father designed it," Kuzen replied.

Thomas crawled forward and slung his feet over the side of the resting spot.

"We can slide down the rest of the way if you like. We've sidestepped all the sharp bits." Kuzen said while adjusting his black wide brimmed hat.

"Let's hurry to the throne room," Thomas replied.

He and Kuzen slid down the remaining seven hundred feet. They dove forward in unison just before reaching the water's edge. The swim to Ungland passed silently. Though the distance was great, neither felt tired as they reached the other side.

They tread water before a tremendous stone block. A short woman sat atop the block and broke off pieces with her hammer and chisel.

"What are you carving?" Thomas asked as he pulled himself from the water.

"Marble," the woman replied.

She kept her eyes on the block and continued chipping.

"Don't you know a battle is coming?" Thomas asked.

The artist laughed and set down her tools. She ran both hands across her block and smiled.

"If I die, I'll die in the pursuit of what means most to me."

Just then, a beanbag chair sized blimp collided with her tits and exploded. Kuzen put his arm around Thomas's shoulder and ran with him into the city.

As the sculptor lay dying, her large, tan lips mouthed, "My king."

Thomas and Kuzen ran down the marble road. An extraordinarily tall man cruised by the end of the path on a flat-bottomed boat.

"Take us to the palace now!" Kuzen screamed.

The tall man took one look at Thomas and bowed low.

"I am honored," he said.

"The feeling is mutual," Thomas replied as he climbed aboard.

Grey blimps circled like vultures. American wheelchair troops rolled from cargo bays and fell into the Unglish Sea. Their chairs sank to the bottom, but their bodies floated. Some were fortunate enough to land with their heads above the water.

The rest floated with their enormous asses exposed. The water level rose with every American dropped.

"They're trying to flood the city and force the King to the top floor of the palace," Kuzen said.

"But I thought they were allies with the king?" Thomas asked.

The owner of the boat looked at Thomas sidelong and raised an eyebrow. He tried to focus on pushing the boat towards the palace with his oaken staff, but could not dispel his confusion. Kuzen put his arm around Thomas's shoulder and whispered.

"The Americans won't have an ally if we reach the King's chambers first. Just watch your tongue until we reach the palace. You never know where a serf's loyalties lie."

Kuzen shifted his eyes towards the tall man.

"Follow my lead and we'll be fine," he continued.

Thomas stared ahead. The water level steadily increased. Unglanders jumped from their windows and climbed the dangling foliage that grew across their homes. Most escaped just as the water poured into their windows.

"They'll lose everything," Thomas said.

"If we don't hurry, they'll suffer worse," Kuzen replied.

"We're almost there," the boatman said while laying his staff by his massive feet.

"Are you tired?" Thomas asked. "I can push us if need be," he added when the boatman did not respond.

"The water is too deep now," Kuzen interrupted.

"Right, my staff won't reach the floor, your m-"

"Jump off!" Kuzen interrupted again.

An American soldier drove over the side of a blimp and crashed into their boat. Her wheel chair snapped the boat in half. The driver fell on his back. Kuzen and Thomas fell into the sea. The boatman pressed his palm against the boat and pushed down with all his might. The American soldier clung to his legs and meant to pull him down with her.

"Why don't you float like the others?" he screamed.

"I've been doing Pilates!" she replied.

"Should we help them?" Thomas asked as he and Kuzen swam towards the palace.

"Help them? I think they make a cute couple," Kuzen replied.

Twenty feet of silver water remained between our heroes and the palace. It was a tall, spiraling building, with an exterior facade constructed entirely of copper. Images of wild beasts and bearded kings stuck out from all sides like three-dimensional copper colored paintings. Thomas reached to touch a lion embossed on the palace wall. The water rose dramatically and his hand fell upon a copper rendering of his own face instead.

"What does this mean?" he asked.

Kuzen pointed at an emerald colored window to his left and replied, "You'll have to look within to know."

Thomas broke the window with his fist. Grey blimps circled the palace, mere inches above the water. A red white and blue hot air balloon with a basket in the shape of a hamburger floated over the palace. A young man in a brown suit stood atop a balcony on the other side. A blonde haired woman looked down at him and could have jumped into the water that bubbled beneath his platform. However, the man she expected to see was not there with him. She pulled a cigarette from her pocket, lit it, then sat down on a beautifully carved chair and drummed her fingernails against the armrest.

13.

Thomas and Kuzen stood at the back end of a tremendous room. Emerald colored windows poured magnificent green light across the floor. Paintings of royalty, displays of precious gems, and miniature carvings of buildings lined the spaces between the windows. A large obsidian stairwell led down into the flooded portion of the palace. A roaring fire gleamed from the golden fireplace on the opposite wall. A young man in a brown coat and brown pants stood directly ahead with his back to our heroes. Thomas opened his mouth to speak, but the young man held up his hand and spoke first.

"I thought I had rid myself of you for good," he said.

Thomas looked over at Kuzen. Kuzen did not say a word.

"But, that's my voice!" Thomas replied.

The young man dressed in brown turned around. Save for the superior state of his clothing, he and Thomas appeared identical.

"Hello Kuzen," the double said while stepping forward so that he and our heroes stood twenty paces apart.

"Do you remember the special gift bestowed onto our family?" the double asked while stepping forward.

Thomas took a step back in perfect time with his double.

"I don't know anything about you!" Thomas replied.

"Odd that," the double remarked. "I am you. Well, you used to be a part of me. Not that it matters if you know. What we used to be no longer exists and you're no more significant than a fingernail to me now," the double said while reaching into his jacket.

He produced a long barreled pistol, and without waiting to say a clever line, shot at Thomas's heart. Kuzen shoved Thomas aside. Thomas struck a bronze pedestal. A wooden carving of a grand cathedral fell from the pedestal and struck Thomas across the back of the head. He held the bloodied carving in his hand.

"I remember this," he whispered.

His attention then turned from the carving to his bloodied hands. He felt the back of his head for a wound and found nothing, then looked over his shoulder and saw Kuzen crawling towards the double.

"Take him back," Kuzen pleaded as he left a bloody trail.

The double replied "No" and fired a second shot. Thomas screamed a "No" that matched the previous in timbre but surpassed it in emotion. Thomas scrambled forward. A flash of light blinded him and his movements became vague. When the flash cleared, a glittering object stood before him. Lord Joseph GobKnobbler the Third stood between Kuzen and the double with Jim Limpdickfaggotballs the Third's head on a platter in his glittering hands. Joseph wore a pink, diamond encrusted singlet. Jim wore a fancy black top hat.

It held the second bullet between his teeth and said, "Hello Thomas!" after spitting the bullet onto the floor.

Its front teeth then shattered and fell onto his plate.

"Hello honey snookums!" Joseph added while winking and ripping a steaming wet fart.

Jim's head twisted from left to right and scrunched up its

nose.

"I do say mein friend. As much gas as you let out in confined areas I'd think you were the German between us!"

Joseph put one hand to his mustache and giggled, releasing tiny aftershock farts with every laugh. Long legged spiders crawled from his nostrils onto his hand. When he replaced his hand onto the plate, Jim's head meant to scream, but its airbag was completely empty.

The double smiled and said, "Well, Uncle, Cousin, old friend, and appendix, if we're done with the pleasantries, I have some people to shoot. Namely, you assholes."

He turned to Joseph and shot; then immediately fired at Jim's head, Kuzen, and Thomas. He expended the final bullet in his six-shooter and cast it at Kuzen's. Like the bullets, the pistol bounced off an invisible wall. Pitre Tumbickler stood before the others, shielding them with a musty wall of his malodorous mime magic.

"What an unexpected visit, cousin Pitre. I didn't even hear you come in," the double said.

Kuzen took his hand from his nose and replied, "That's because he's a mime you stupid ass!"

Blood leaked between his teeth as he spoke. He pressed his hands against the invisible wall and propped himself upwards. Thomas ran forward and allowed Kuzen to lean on his left shoulder. Pitre's gigantic gastrointestinal gust slowed to a mere whistle. He blushed through his white makeup and pulled a wheel of cheese from his pocket.

"Need to reload?" Kuzen asked.

Pitre nodded. Joseph took a step forward and breathed in deeply the bountiful bouquet of Pitre's pungently permeating poo perfume. He placed Jim's head onto the floor then pulled a quill and parchment from the back of his singlet. He wrote his number on the paper and handed it to Pitre, then put his hand to the side of his head as though holding a phone and mouthed, "Call me." Pitre glanced at the number and shrugged. Joseph blushed from his nipples to the top of his head and pressed Pitre's hands to his chest.

"I mean, text me."

Thomas and Kuzen took five steps forward.

"We're almost there," Kuzen said.

His voice sounded deeper than usual. Blood dripped from the hole in his stomach.

"Are you ready to tell me what this is all about?" Thomas asked.

"Just reach out and touch him," Kuzen replied.

The double backed onto his balcony. He grabbed a shield from the wall and tossed it at Thomas. A flash of fur flew between Thomas and his double. The shield fell to the ground in several pieces.

"That counts!" a high-pitched voice cried.

"What counts?" Kuzen asked.

Havana Gila stood off to the side with a sword in hand, a beautiful new nose, and a very small band-aid on what remained of his penis. Water gurgled in the stairwell behind him, then began to recede.

"That goy hat rack promised me fifteen percent of Poland if I helped."

"We agreed on ten percent!" Jim's head mouthed in vain.

Havana saw he had the upper hand and smiled.

"The man threw a shield. I cut it down, therefore I helped."

Havana smiled and ran past the double. He stood at the edge of the balcony and waved.

"I'll stop over for my twenty percent later!" he screamed before leaping over the edge.

Two seconds later, Havana screamed "Oy vey!" and bounced back into view. A red white and blue blimp ascended above the balcony. Havana tumbled over the top and fell into the receding sea. A blonde woman stood atop the hamburger shaped basket dangling from the blimp. She took her hands from the controls and left the balloon to hover in mid air. She then kicked open the basket door and stepped onto the platform.

"I never said you could kill him," she said.

"I… I'm sorry master," the double replied.

He went to his knees and tried to take the woman's hand.

"Please forgive me Hillary I didn't know you still cared," he pleaded.

Kuzen pulled his hat backwards so the brim no longer obscured his face. Burned out youth stretched across his wrinkled forehead and tightly drawn cheeks.

"It's been a long time Chilly," he said.

Hillary ignored Kuzen and trained her eyes on Thomas.

"Do you remember me?" she asked.

"I remember you pointing a gun at me in America," Thomas said while taking one step forward.

Hillary reached into her dark blue dress and felt that very same pistol in her hand. For the time being, she decided not to use it.

"I mean, do you remember meeting me two and a half years ago?" she asked.

Thomas did not respond. The double sunk lower to the floor so that he was practically on his stomach.

"You were once the proud and noble King of Ungland. Well, you were for a couple of weeks following your father's sudden death abroad. I had long awaited the chance to take your throne. Thanks to your weakness, I found that chance."

Hillary curtsied and held out her right hand. The double fell to his knees and kissed Hillary's wrinkled fingers.

"I don't remember any of that," Thomas replied.

"That makes sense," Hillary said as she glared at the double and withdrew her hand. "It wasn't you that surrendered to me after all. It was this other Thomas Dublin."

"Dublin?" Thomas asked. "Is that my last name?"

"No," the double replied. "It is MY name. YOU are

nothing but a shadow, the half remembered imprint of a misplaced dream."

"Explain it to him," Hillary said.

The double took a deep breath.

"Explain!" Hillary demanded.

Joseph leaned against Pitre's shoulder and attempted to whisper. He was poor at the craft and whispered loudly instead.

"What an annoying cunt. I hope she catches her beef lips in the zipper of that ugly pants suit the next time she squats down to lay a clutch of eggs."

Hillary glared at Pitre. Pitre smiled and continued to eat his cheese. A red white and blue helicopter hovered by the balcony, but Hillary waved it away. The helicopter pilot reached his hand out of the window to give his president a thumbs up. His swollen thumb struck the helicopter blade, flew through the air, and landed between Joseph's breasts.

He dropped it into the back of his singlet and whispered, "I'll save this plump partner for later."

Hillary kicked the double in the ribs. He glared at Thomas and began to speak.

"Our family's gift is a blessing for one of us and a curse for the other. When a Dublin's life is threatened, the weakness that threatens his survival is expelled like a spider casting off its worn and withered skin. When Hillary's army attacked through the mountains, we had no means of defense. She held our people hostage and threatened to kill them if I did not submit. You wanted to fight. You insisted on fighting to our last. I cast that part of myself aside and kneeled at Hillary's feet. I have suffered that shame for my people. Though they may become as infantile and ignorant as the Americans, they will at least survive!"

"That is enough," Hillary said as she kicked the double in the face.

He went completely limp. Silent tears welled in his bloodshot eyes.

"Leave him alone," Thomas commanded.

"Oh, such a demanding little boy," Hillary said while stepping forward. "Why, three years ago, you were like putty in my hand."

She put her hand to her mouth and laughed.

"Of course, that goes for you too Kuzen."

Kuzen wanted to speak, but blood filled his mouth and he spat at Hillary's opened toed sandals instead.

"What do you mean?" Thomas replied.

"After the split, you were soft and pink, like a new born penis. I knew I had to take you hostage. With the rightful king of Ungland in my keeping, no Yuropean nation would dare to touch me. With you as my chess piece, my rise to power was nearly secured. However, you awoke from your stupor and tried to shove me over the side of the hot air balloon parked behind us. Isn't it a lovely vessel? Kuzen and I first kissed upon it."

"Kissed?" Thomas asked while turning back towards Kuzen.

"That vile bitch," he spat. "I climbed that mountain every day hoping to find a path to the outside world. It took me years just to find the door to the cave. I followed those caverns forward and backwards until my blisters bled. The king beneath the stones taunted me, leading me each hour towards destruction. When I had just lost hope, I saw her floating over the top in her hot air balloon. She wore some kind high tech mesh suit that made her look young and beautiful."

"I still am," Hillary interjected.

"Honey," Kuzen replied. "Right now, I'd rather jam my cock in the British poof behind me."

"That can be arranged," Joseph and Hillary replied in unison.

Kuzen grimaced and fell towards Thomas. Thomas took another step back and propped Kuzen against his shoulder.

"How could you trust her?" Thomas asked.

"I was young, naive, and exceptionally horny. She was the first girl I had ever met that wasn't a first cousin, and also the first blonde I had ever seen. The gene pool in Ungland is two feet deep and I tired of only getting my ankles wet."

Kuzen turned to his right and peered into Thomas's hazel eyes.

"She used me. After several weeks, we found a way through the mountains together. We spent the night on the Polish side of the border making love through the holes in her false costume. She awoke before me and led the old world American army to this palace."

"Then what?" Hillary asked with a grin.

"You shot me in the leg!" Kuzen replied.

Hillary pulled the pistol from her dress and tossed it at Kuzen's foot.

"That's the one alright," Kuzen rasped.

A long trickle of blood fell from his mouth as he continued to speak.

"Four bullets ruined my right leg. I fled up and through the mountains, chasing after that damned burger blimp. By the time I reached Poland, I was crippled for life." he said.

"There's still one bullet left in that gun. If you're so depressed you're more than welcome to use it."

Kuzen put one arm around Thomas's shoulder and pushed the other against the wall.

"Then use it on yourself you dirty bitch!" Kuzen replied.

He pulled back his remaining leg and kicked the pistol at Hillary. She grabbed it in mid air and fired. Kuzen meant to push Thomas aside but Thomas acted first. He shoved Kuzen to the ground and sprang forward. Hillary's bullet passed through Thomas's left shoulder. He continued forward and fell to the ground inches from his double.

"I'm coming home," Thomas said.

"I'm so sorry," the double replied.

Their hands touched, like perfect reflections of a single point of light. Memories, old friends, a beloved father, and an absent mother popped into Thomas's mind. As much as he suddenly recalled, there was much more that he wanted to know, more than he ever originally knew. Thomas and the double sparked crimson flames like twin piles of ash in a furnace. The fires grew into one tremendous blue inferno. Though the flame licked Hillary and the palace interior, it was cold to the touch and produced no outer effect. The flame fell dim and diminished. King Thomas Dublin the Third stood before Hillary Clinton and the friends that had gathered to save his land.

His old brown suit hung in tatters on his body but he paid that little mind.

"Hillary, leave this land now while you can do so under your own power," he commanded.

"And why the hell should I?" Hillary demanded to know.

She reached into the top of her outfit and grasped a shoulder pad.

From the pad, she retrieved a transceiver and growled, "Begin the final stage of the attack."

The person receiving the message took a long sip from a container of soda and burped before replying, "Yes mom. I mean, Miss President Mom, I mean, mam that is totally not like a mom to me. Oh god I'm sorry please don't take away my pokem-."

Hillary shook her head and clicked off the transceiver. Hundreds of red white and blue helicopters descended from the skies. Their beating blades shook the emerald windows of the palace until they shattered. Golden light poured into the palace hall. Thomas approached Hillary and pushed her back into a pedestal, then reached behind Hillary and flipped over a wooden statue of the palace. He pressed a silver button on the underside and smiled.

"What the hell do you think you're doing?" Hillary asked

while trying to shove Thomas away.

"I'm keeping a promise I made to myself just now. To never forget what I cherish and to protect it always. My other half may have surrendered the country, but he never gave up on our architectural designs."

A sensor in the button read Thomas's thumbprint and sent a signal to every spire in Ungland. The ornate spire tops spiraled open like onions discarding their peels. Massive cannons rotated out of the shadowy canopies and shot down the American helicopters. Explosions rocked the palace and every statue toppled to the floor. Thomas stared into Hillary's eyes as a flaming helicopter nearly collided with Hillary's hot air balloon.

"This means nothing," Hillary said.

She ducked under Thomas's arm and sprinted for her balloon.

"Please wait!" Kuzen cried.

Blood dripped from his outstretched hand. Hillary stood upon the hamburger shaped basket and watched Kuzen with downcast eyes.

"Neither of us kept the promise we made in Poland. Though, I'm glad to see you still wear the hat I gave you," she said with a sideways grin.

"It's because of you my hair's falling out," Kuzen replied while throwing his hat aside.

His hand fell limp and struck the floor. Thomas and the other reinstated kings rushed to help him, save for Jim's head. Jim's head just kind of watched from afar.

"Kuzen!" Hillary cried as her balloon ascended. "The love we had was real. But it is dead and gone forever. Next we meet, I'll likely k-"

Hillary was denied the chance to finish her sentence. Havana Gila pounced on top of her balloon and pierced it with the remaining portion of his penis.

He laughed maniacally and screamed, "Tell it to your book club you stuck up goy dyke!"

The hot air balloon swerved to the left as air shot from the punctured side. It then rose, shifted to the right, slammed the basket against the balcony, and finally fell into the sea. Havana jumped onto the balcony and pointed to Jim.

"Now I'll take twenty five percent and a nice vacation home in Florida," he wailed.

"Get the fuck off my land!" Thomas interjected.

"No prob, Bob," Havana replied.

He then clicked his heels and dove into the sea.

"He knows the water level dropped right?" Joseph asked.

"That doesn't matter," Thomas replied. "You and Pitre run downstairs and fetch the doctor. His office is down the main hallway through the double blue doors. If he isn't there, grab some supplies and hurry back!"

Joseph and Pitre ran off as directed.

"So you really do remember," Kuzen said with some difficulty.

"I remember my old friend Kuzen that used to live with me like a brother. The very same Kuzen that taught me how to read and accidentally stabbed me with a pen while we played at being knights."

"And do you remember what I said to you the day the Americans invaded?"

"You ran off with that ruined leg and promised to make things right. I never thought you could recover my other half. Despite the change caused by the split, I always hoped you would."

Kuzen's eyes went wide. He pointed at a bearded man in a black suit staring at him from down a hallway.

"It's him, my other half. I left him in that mountain passage and now he's come back to kill me!" Kuzen screamed.

Thomas ran at the man with his fists drawn and collided with something that shattered.

"What the hell?" Thomas asked.

"That's just my reflection in your mother's old mirror you idiot! You were always forgetting about your mother," Kuzen said while laughing.

"That's right," Thomas said. "I never knew anything about her."

He cast his eyes upon the shattered remnants of his mother's mirror and suddenly wished he could see just one fragment of her reflection.

"Aha," Kuzen said while holding a bloody finger in the air. "When I'm well enough to talk, we can discuss my last encounter with the absent Queen."

Pitre and Joseph returned with a wheelchair and an entire team of doctors. Thomas backed away to give them access to Kuzen, then approached the balcony where his father used to bounce him on his knee.

"Where is my mother? Is she alive? Is my father really dead?" he thought aloud.

Loud rumbling interrupted his thoughts. The hamburger shaped basket from Hillary's blimp ascended on twelve mighty rocket thrusters. Hillary's hair hung in tangled locks and her blue dress shimmered with Unglish water.

"This is not over yet Thomas Dublin!" she shrieked. "I am going on a tour across the world to gather allies. I'll be back in a month with more man power than even you can manage!"

She breathed heavily and grit her teeth. Glaring over Thomas's shoulder; her eyes met Kuzen's. An unspoken message passed between them. Whether her parting words were a warning or a threat, Thomas would not be able to tell.

"And don't you get comfortable before then, the Russians have observed our encounter. They know your defenses now and are likely preparing to attack."

"Tell me," Thomas cried before Hillary flew away. "Why does everyone want my land?"

If Hillary answered, the rocket thrusters of her basket drowned out her reply. Kuzen rolled to Thomas in his wheel chair. A doctor followed him closely and continued to stitch his wound.

"Why should the world covet such a tiny crust of land

like Ungland?" Thomas asked.

Kuzen grasped his hat from the floor and set it on his lap as he watched Hillary fly away.

"Because my friend," Kuzen replied. "The enslaved will always begrudge a man that is free."

Also by Michael Saint Wood:

Yurope 2: Barack's Apocalypse   [Black Comedy]
http://www.amazon.com/dp/B00QEFKE60

What if Trayvon Martin survived and George Zimmerman died in his place? What if President Barack Obama accidentally released a chemical agent that turns African American's into super powered stereotypes? Would the world come to a horrific end? Trayvon Martin, Michael Brown, President Barack Obama, Jesse Jackson and dozens of other real life pillars of the black community meet and clash in this satirical prequel to Yurope! Hillary's Invasion.

Split in Two   [Surreal Mystery]
https://www.amazon.com/dp/B00KO51BOK

From the author of Yurope! Hillary's Invasion and Yurope 2: Barack's Apocalypse comes Split in Two, a surreal mystery set in the rainy town of Voorhees. Split in Two is told from the perspective of a man who's wife has vanished. In his seclusion, Jonathan has built a world for himself, from himself. Whether his wife has skipped town, or if another person has taken her place, he can no longer tell. Whether he follows her shadow towards paradise or ruin, John is too exhausted to care. Split in Two blends horror and mystery while challenging the concept of identity, not only of one's loved one's, but also of one's self.

This book is licensed for your personal enjoyment only. If you did not enjoy it, you may still retain the license, you awful excuse for a human being. This book may not be resold or given away to other people, not even your mom. If you would like to share this book with another person, please purchase an additional copy for each recipient or stand atop a building a read it via a bullhorn. If someone tries to make you stop, throw the bullhorn at them and continue screaming. If you're reading

this book and did not purchase it, or it was not purchased for your use only, I just hope you enjoyed it and maybe tell a friend about it. Thank you for respecting the comparatively hard work of the author.

Made in the USA
Coppell, TX
18 February 2021